D1291553

GAY
for my
BAE

KEESHIA K.

By KEESHIA K.

ARE YOU ON OUR EMAIL LIST?

SIGN UP ON OUR WEBSITE

www.thecartelpublications.com

OR TEXT THE WORD:

CARTELBOOKS TO 22828

FOR PRIZES, CONTESTS, ETC.

CHECK OUT OTHER TITLES BY THE CARTEL PUBLICATIONS

4   *By KEESHIA K.*

GAY FOR MY BAE 5

By KEESHIA K.

Gay For My Bae

By
Keeshia K.

Library of Congress Control Number: 2018935684

ISBN 10: 1948373181

ISBN 13: 978-1948373180

Cover Design: Bookslutgirl.com

www.thecartelpublications.com
First Edition
Printed in the United States of America

By KEESHIA K.

What's Up Fam,

Wow, there have been so many changes and happenings since my last letter. Too many to actually roll call at the moment but I will say this, please make sure you take care of yourself, spiritually, mentally, emotionally and physically. This world we live in can get crazy and we need to make sure that we are prepared as much as we can be to take it on.

Now that the heavy stuff is out the way, let me get into the book in hand, "Gay For My Bae". This novel was a fun and crazy read. It reminds me that you MUST be careful what you wish for because you just might get it. I really enjoyed reading this one and I know you will too!

With that being said, keeping in line with tradition, we want to give respect to a vet or trailblazer paving the way. In this novel, we would like to recognize:

Jonathan Abrams

Jonathan Abrams is an American journalist and author of my new favorite book, "All The Pieces Matter: The Inside Story of The Wire". Anyone who knows me knows that, THE WIRE, is one of my ABSOLUTE favorite TV shows ever. The book that Jonathan Abrams wrote breaks down The Wire by giving us behind the scenes information told by the writers, cast members and crew of the show. I am a huge fan and what this book proved to me was, you can never know all there is to know. If you are a fan of The Wire, this book is a MUST READ. If you haven't seen The Wire, then read this book first and then check it out! You won't be disappointed.

Aight, get to it. I'll catch you in the next book.

Be Easy!

Charisse "C. Wash" Washington
Vice President
The Cartel Publications
www.thecartelpublications.com
www.facebook.com/publishercwash
Instagram: publishercwash
www.twitter.com/cartelbooks
www.facebook.com/cartelpublications
Follow us on Instagram: Cartelpublications
#CartelPublications
#UrbanFiction
#PrayForCeCe
#PrayForT
#JonathanAbrams

CARTEL URBAN CINEMA'S WEB SERIES

BMORE CHICKS

@ Pink Crystal Inn

NOW AVAILABLE:

Via

YOUTUBE

And

DVD

(Season 2 Coming Soon)

www.youtube.com/user/tstyles74

www.cartelurbancinema.com

www.thecartelpublications.com

#GayForMyBae

By KEESHIA K.

CHAPTER ONE

TAEVONNE

"I knew this nigga was gonna do me dirty," I thought as I tried my hardest to stop more urine from trickling into my draws.

We should've just gone to the JOP to get married. At least then, if he pulled this stunt I wouldn't be standing at the alter solo looking dumb as shit.

"Um, Ms. Colby, I have another wedding to perform in thirty minutes." Reverend Miles whispered to me across the alter. "What would you like to do?" He asked.

How the fuck do I know? I thought. He acted as if I had him somewhere hidden and didn't want the room full of guests who were waiting on me to see him.

"Baby, you want me to go see where this dude at?" My father walked up to me and asked. I could tell he was embarrassed for me, and it only made me feel even worse.

"No, I...I'll go," I told him as I farted thinking about this walk of shame I'm getting ready to take. I handed my red rose bouquet to my girl Stacy. She looked like she wanted to throw up as she took it from me.

What the fuck was your face screwed up for? You ain't the one in the wedding gown, bitch. I thought mad about it all. You also ain't the one who has to take the walk of 'No Groom' shame.

I turned around facing the semi crowded church. I lifted the train of my dress up so I wouldn't trip and headed to the back of the building. As I pushed down the aisle, I refused to look at the faces of my family and friends. I ain't need no more pity. What fucking good would that do me?

I finally made it to the back when all of a sudden, I felt like I was about to pass out. I needed to get some fresh air and gather my thoughts. If I didn't I knew I was about to suffer one of the many panic attacks that had stricken me all of my life.

I pushed open the church doors and my stomach flipped at what I saw outside. My fiancé'. He was sitting down fully dressed in his sexy navy blue tuxedo smoking a Capone. From the back I was looking at his fresh haircut and his broad shoulders that hugged me this morning saying he was proud he was going to be my husband.

"Bronco, what's going on? Why you out here instead of inside? You know what time it is right?" My voice was really low at first and I wondered if he heard what I said.

He looked up at me. "Tae, we need to talk." Bronco said ignoring all of my questions. He took a deep breath and turned around to look at me.

"Now, you wanna talk now?" I looked behind me. "I mean, we supposed to be in there saying I do." I told him. "We supposed to be in there getting ready to start the rest of our lives together. We supposed to be…married."

"You not fucking hearing me, Tae!" He yelled and I jumped. "I'm not going in there to say shit until we have words." He shot back tapping his Capone to drop the ashes too hard on the wall, causing it to fall to the ground.

I took a deep breath and walked over to the bench he sat on. I hiked up my white wedding gown as much ass possible and sat next to him. He looked over at me, then back out into the street before he spoke. It was like my life flashed before my eyes and he hadn't said word one.

God, please don't let this man walk out of my life. I'd sooner run in front of an eighteen-wheeler before I let him go.

"Tae, I been thinking 'bout this shit for a while and I can't marry you like this." He started.

My eyes fluttered rapidly and my heart rate increased. It was like I was looking at someone else's life and not my own. "But you asked me to...I thought you loved me." I said. "You...you got down on your

By KEESHIA K.

knee in front of my parents and yours and said you wanted *me*. Remember?" I had to fight back tears because if I cried my makeup would get ruined. What was I thinking? This man was about to leave. What do I care how I look?

"I do. Love ain't got nothing to do with it." He paused and reached into his pocket to grab the box of Capones. I slapped it out of his hand.

"Then what is it?" I questioned. "I need to know right now!"

"It's just…I mean, I—" He stuttered.

If this nigga don't spit it out, I'm gonna strangle him right here in front of God's house. I thought. If I was gonna die from embarrassment he would die at my hands.

I looked at him harder to try and read his face.

Ohhhh…He was scared to tell me. I needed to put his ass at ease so he could say what was on his mind. So I grabbed his hand and looked into his hazel eyes.

"Bae...Talk to me." I took a deep breath. "Whatever it is we can make it through it." I assured him. "Please."

"Whatever it is?" He said. "No matter what?"

"No matter what."

He exhaled deeply. "I need variety." He said.

"Huh?"

"What I mean is, I can be your husband but, I'ma need to mix it up in our bedroom sexually or I can't go through with the wedding." He paused. "I mean, I never stepped out on you except two times but I'm saying even that won't be enough. If I'm gonna be your husband you gotta give me the okay to go after more."

Was this bamma serious? "So what does that mean?" I asked puzzled.

"From time to time, in order for me to be satisfied and stay happy, we gonna need to bring in different women to fuck." He said boldly. "But the thing is I'm

By KEESHIA K.

not no selfish ass nigga. I want you to have fun too by being with them."

I was shocked. "So let me get this straight, you wanna be able to sleep with other women?" I asked needing clarity. "In our bedroom? In front of me?"

He took a deep breath, grabbed the box of Capones off the ground and lit another one. I let him. "Yeah, but like I said since you'd be my wife, we'd sleep with them together and bae, it'll be so much fun. All I'm asking you is to trust me." He stared into my eyes. "You do that and I'll walk in there right now and give you my last name." He paused. "So, what you gonna do?" He took a pull and exhaled.

CHAPTER TWO

TAE

"Throw your legs over my shoulders." My new husband demanded as he power drove his extra hard dick into my dripping wet pussy. We may have had our differences sometimes but there was no denying that he knew how to handle my body and me. We were at the Fiesta Americana Grand Coral Beach Resort in Cancun Mexico on our honeymoon and I was in heaven.

Yes. I married him and before you say anything, hear me out. I had been dating Bronco for five years before he even thought about proposing to me. He was my life. My breath and the reason for doing even the smallest of things in my world. And there was no way in hell I was giving up my man over a simple request that he may or may not even follow through with. Besides, as long as I reminded him how good being with me felt then I should be fine.

I mean look at us, we were at this beautiful resort in a suite over looking the blue ocean and my husband, not my boyfriend is fucking the shit outta me. From my view I could see the palm trees swaying and even hear the rush of the water slapping against the beach while he slapped my ass.

"Mmmmmmmm, take this pussy, bae! It's all yours." I told him as I grabbed my ankles and opened my legs wider. "Mmmm...deeper, deeper," I moaned. "Give it to me just like that."

"Got damn right this my pussy!" He said. I could see him biting his lip so hard I thought it would bleed. "Get them legs open...wider. Sssssss, mmmmmmh, oh shit! It's so fucking wet." He lowered his body and whispered in my ear. "I'm beating this up all night too." He continued as he swirled his hips around hitting my spot. "Bounce on it." He told me as he gripped me by my shoulders and flipped over. Now I was on top. "Yep, ride that shit just like that. Look at them titties jumping. Fuck!"

He knew that shit drove me crazy. Some bitches don't like riding niggas but I lived for it. It made me feel in control and I always cum harder from up there. Maybe it was the way he looked up under me. Or how is eyes got lower with each hop. Who knows? All I can confirm is that our sex life was right.

When I started getting in my rhythm I began to wind my hips. He could never last long when I did this shit so I closed my eyes and made sure I was close to my climax too. "I'm almost there, zaddy," I said. "Just...just don't stop please."

"Give me them titties!" He said as he sat up and grabbed my left breast and circled his tongue around my nipple lightly while he pumped up and down inside me. "Look at you up there looking all pretty and shit."

Suddenly my cream slid down his shaft and soaked his thighs as I screamed out my orgasm. It was the hardest I ever came and I wanted to return the favor. So when I felt his dick pulsating, I immediately jumped up to give him part two of his treat. I grabbed the shaft and licked around the tip while using my right hand to jerk him rapidly. "Cum for me baby." I said before shoving all of him in my mouth. "I wanna feel that shit sliding down my throat."

When he got louder and his body tightened up I knew that did it. He grabbed the sides of my head and squeezed his ass harder while he shot his load down into my esophagus. It was a lot too, which shocked me because we'd been fucking non-stop since we arrived yesterday.

"Ahhhhhh...Damn baby! If I'da known you'd be fucking me like this, I'da married you years ago. Shit." He said to me while huffing and puffing out of breath. "Girl, what you trying to do to me? Make me marry that ass again?" He laughed.

"Nah, you already got this. I just want you to see what you been missing before you made me your wife." I said as I rolled over and wiped the sides of my mouth. I layed on my side and faced him. He was still trying to catch his breath. "You ready for another round?" I teased him. "Because shit about to change in the bedroom. You sure you can handle me?"

"Girl, you gonna drain me dry." He laughed. "But give me an hour to recharge and I got you. Trust me." He stated. He held out his arm and I slid over to lie on his chest and shut my eyes.

It was like I was trying to freeze this moment in time. Suddenly I wasn't concerned about him wanting another woman. Shit, he couldn't even handle me. Yeah, we were going to have the best marriage ever. I could already see it.

THE NEXT MORNING

Horny as ever when I woke up, I rolled over in our King-sized bed to the sounds of the ocean waves crashing onto the beach. I tried to curl up under Bronco before waking him for round two before breakfast. But when I got over to his side of the bed, it was cool. He wasn't there.

By KEESHIA K.

I opened my eyes and looked around the room. "Bronco," I called out for him assuming he was in the bathroom. No answer. "Bae, don't try to hide from me." I said playfully. "I'ma get at that again for sure."

I climbed out of the bed, my feet slapped on the cold marble floor. I was still butt naked from our all night love making sessions and saw no use for clothes. Besides, we were in Mexico. Still searching, I walked around our suite and before long noticed that his wallet and key card were gone. "Maybe he went down to eat without me." I said to myself. Besides, Mexico was gorgeous so I couldn't blame him.

I decided to go down and join him. It was a beautiful day out and I needed to soak up some of this sun before life got back to normal at home. But before that I needed to wash my ass. I'm sure nobody wanted to be sitting across from a big cum bucket at breakfast.

When I got down to the buffet, I scanned the room looking for Bronco. I didn't see him anywhere in the room and things weren't making sense. *Maybe he ate and was already on the beach.* I thought. He loved swimming in the ocean so I'm sure he was out there somewhere I just had to find him. I wished he was courteous enough to have left me a note, but whatever.

Although I was starving, before I grabbed any food, I wanted to find him. I walked out the dining room area and onto the pool deck. It was about 10:00 o'clock in the morning but there were quite a few people out enjoying the pool. As I rounded the corner I saw a man across the deck in the hot tub that looked like Bronco from behind. The sun was so bright that even with my MCM shades on, I couldn't get a good look. Especially since the guy had his back toward me.

When I got closer, and walked around I saw that it was Bronco soaking in the Jacuzzi. He had his arms outstretched across the tub with his head leaned back. My nigga was so damn fine and I took a second to admire the view before alerting him I was there. His honey brown skin was now sun kissed and all his tattoo's seemed to come alive across is back. He looked so relaxed.

I decided to creep up to surprise him.

"Heyyyyy husband...the fuck!" I shouted as I walked up and saw some random bitch with his dick in her mouth. She pulled back in shock when she saw the heat in my face and wiped the corners of her lips. "What...what...what's going on?" It felt like the breath had been kicked out of me with a boot.

"Tae! What the fuck you doing out here?" He had the nerve to ask me like I was the one out there getting topped off. "Why you ain't...I'm saying...I was gonna come get you later!"

"What?" I yelled still in shock holding my chest.

"You heard me," he yelled scrambling out of the Jacuzzi. Walking toward his trunks he grabbed them off a lawn chair and reached for his towel. The woman snatched her towel off the deck, slithered out and scurried off like the whore she was.

"I...I can't believe you did this to me! I can't believe...after everything you...you doing this!" I looked around and saw that a lot of people watched our little movie unfold. I was so embarrassed and realized I was being made a fool of so with my heart broken I stormed off.

"The fuck was you doing creeping up on me?" Bronco asked as he walked into our hotel room. He tossed the wet towel on the floor and stomped up to me. "Trying to be sneaky and shit." He said through clenched teeth.

Was I having a nightmare? He gets caught cheating and he goes off on me? "How can you ask me some shit like that?" I yelled in tears. "I woke up and you were gone, Bronco! I came downstairs to join you thinking you were eating. I ain't know you'd be all out in the open fucking some skank!"

By KEESHIA K.

"What you tripping for? I mean, don't act like you wasn't hip. What the fuck you think I was talking about outside the church? Huh?" He asked. "See, I knew you couldn't handle this shit. Can't believe I went through with it. Something told me not to marry you and I did it anyway." He shot back. Every word he yelled felt like daggers into my heart. But he was doing the most. So I had to gather his things.

"Bronco, I remember everything you said. You specifically told me if I agreed it would be us together. Not you by yourself without my knowledge. Those were your rules not mine. And already you breaking them and blaming me! How could you?" I threw his own words back into his face.

He looked puzzled and stuck. "You know what...this shit dumb." He scratched his head. "I ain't 'bout to sit up in here arguing with you. If you can't handle me getting a 'lil head on vacay out the country, how the hell you gonna handle this marriage? If anything that was a test and guess what? You failed!" He said before he grabbed his key card again and walked back out the door.

"What have I set myself up for?" I said as I flopped down onto the bed and cried into my hands. I grew up with a mother and father who were still in love to this day. Them being together and happy were the only pictures I ever had of marriage but mine looks nothing like theirs. Bronco is so hateful and angry that it makes me wonder if his purpose in life is to break me down, not love me.

Dear, God! What was I gonna do?

By KEESHIA K.

CHAPTER THREE

TAE

This was the kind of thing that bothered me to no end, even though I know it's the least of my problems. I mean, why does he not dry the floor after he stepped out of the shower, dripping wet? Now my socks are soaked and...

What was I talking about? Really the only thing that was on my mind was that Bronco and me hadn't spoken since we left Mexico and I was worried beyond all worry that he would leave me. And although my head said it could be a good thing, I couldn't see it.

Taking a deep breath I removed my wet socks and tossed them into the hamper. Now back home in our apartment in Hyattsville Maryland and all I had to show for our vacation was a broken heart. Normally, Bronco not speaking to me for a few days wouldn't bother me so bad. I would just make his favorite meal and everything would be cool but now I didn't know what to do.

Since it was my off day and Bronco was at work, I asked my BEST, Stacy, to swing by and chill with me. She usually knew what to say to get me in a better mood and we had so much to catch up on. To be honest we hadn't really rapped since my wedding and I had a lot to fill her in about.

Part of me was nervous about telling her everything. I mean, I know how Bronco and my situation looked to me so saying it out loud to someone else would be crazy. I couldn't even wrap my mind around the fact that I had given him the okay to be with other women. On the other hand, Stacy was my BITCH so I must keep it one hundred with her. Plus I needed to get this shit off my chest or I was sure I was gonna die.

By KEESHIA K.

"So, love, how was Mexico?" Stacy asked me. She was a big pretty girl with dark skin and red locs. She was sitting on my couch with me drinking her favorite cocktail, Hennessy with a shot of Hennessy.

"Mmmmmm, girl it was beautiful," I said as I faked a smile. "I mean the weather was gorgeous every day we were there and the water was ice blue and warm. Oh, and the people were so sweet. I could have stayed forever." I explained. "Have you ever been?"

"Chile, bye, you know I can't leave the country." She confessed. "Not the way my parole is set up." She laughed. "But I'm glad you had a good time. Because let's be clear, this means for better or worse. Ain't no turning around now."

"Well, when you can, honey, I suggest you get a passport and go," I said ignoring her little remark about my marriage. "It is truly a must see." I continued.

She looked at me suspiciously. "Yeah...Yeah...Yeah, but I'm surprised you saw anybody's ocean. Because, if

I know you, ya'll was all over each other the whole time." She said sarcastically.

"Yeah, something like that." A picture of him getting his dick sucked in the Jacuzzi ran through my mind.

"But truth be told, I'm shocked ya'll even made it to Mexico, honey. The way you was standing up at that alter by yourself sweating. Ohhhh, I felt so bad for my girl." She shuddered. "My heart was palpitating so fiercely. You don't know how happy I was seeing ya'll two walk back into that church together, I'm trying to tell you." She stated. "It wasn't just me either."

"Yeah, the whole clapping when we came back in made shit more awkward but I was just happy we were together." I sat quietly and debated whether to spill my tea or not.

She sipped her drink. I watched how she took another huge gulp and placed the glass back down on the table. The glass looked so tiny in her large hand. Let me give you a little background so I can get my mind off my own shit for a moment. Stacy was 'Trans', although it was hard to tell upon first glance.

She was beautiful, but shit, she was always beautiful. Even as a boy. We grew up together and she was always her own person, something I wished I could be. That's what I loved most about her. But about five years ago, she fell deep into depression. And in order to pull herself out, she decided to be honest about who she was and live her best life. That's when she threw the whole boy away and my best friend Stanley became my best friend Stacy.

That shit took so much courage to do. I really did admire her bravery and I hoped that one day, if need be, I would have it in me to be just as brave.

"Helllloooo..." Stacy yelled snapping her fingers. "Come back, baby. The plane done landed. We not in Mexico anymore." She joked.

I chuckled.

"So, tell me...how was the *husband* dick, girl?" She asked. "I mean was it the same as boyfriend dick?

What, chile…Do speak! The suspense is killing me over here!"

"Well, when we first got there it was non-stop sex." I cleared my throat. "But, then we got into a fight. A bad one." I confessed.

"What? Why?" She inquired.

"'Cuz I found him in the hot tub getting his dick sucked by another bitch." I admitted reluctantly.

"Shut…the…fuck…up!" She roared. "You have gotta be kidding me! On your honeymoon?" She asked.

"I sooo wish I was playing but I'm not." I could feel myself about to cry and tried my best to calm down. "Nope, I caught him, on day two of our trip. And to make matters worse he didn't even care, Stacy. He just…he was just so mean."

"Oh, soooo when are we having the divorce party?" She asked me seriously. "Because it's one thing to stall on your wedding day but now he adding a second bitch on your honeymoon too?"

"I don't want to divorce him, Stac!" I confessed. "Plus, I have to tell you something else that may make all of this make sense." I wiped the tears that crept down my face. "You may...you may give me some other advice on what I can do to keep him."

She bugged her eyes out and stared at me intensely waiting for my confession. "What you can do to keep him? Have you officially lost your mind? Is that man knocking you in the head or something?"

"Just listen, please." I took a deep breath. "On the day of my wedding, when I went out to find Bronco, he was sitting outside. He told me he couldn't marry me unless I agreed that we would bring women into our bed." I said as I looked down at my feet then back up at her.

She covered her mouth. "Oh my fucking God!" She said through her fingers. "I can't believe what I'm hearing. You...you gave him a pass for some additional ass?"

I nodded my head.

"Taevonne Alexus Colby...Why would you go into a marriage that started off with a stipulation like that?" She asked standing up in front of me. "What on earth is wrong with you? Because I know Mr. and Mrs. Colby didn't raise you on stupid."

"I ain't have no choice." I said looking up at her. "He wasn't going to marry me and I...I need him."

"Why didn't you refuse? Why didn't you give him an ultimatum? I mean did he hold a gun to your head too?" She asked.

"Yeah, kinda. At least that's how it felt in my mind. I mean what else was I supposed to do, not get married? I had a church full of people who were ready to put my embarrassment on Snap." I said. "And I...I love him."

She looked down at me and shook her head slowly from left to right. "That's exactly what the fuck you do! Of course people would have been shady, that's what they do, but at least you could have your self-dignity about you. Now look. It hadn't even been a week and already the man stepped outside of your marriage."

I knew she was right but suddenly I grew angry. "I got my dignity! I didn't tell you my truth so you could come in here and make me feel bad about my decision." I shouted feeling slightly embarrassed that I even opened my mouth.

"Trick, you told me because you knew I would give it to you raw." She pointed at me with her long blue nail. "And you told me because deep in that brain of yours you know I'm right." She boasted.

Fuck that! She ain't my mother. "You know what, I'ma need you to bounce." I told her standing up, crossing my arms over my chest. "I don't have time to sit here and be looked down on for marrying the man I love." I continued. "This is between me and him."

"Honey, if he was a real man who truly loved you, he would have never pulled up on you with that bullshit." She reached down and yanked her purse off the couch and threw it over her shoulder.

"Bye, Stacy." I said firmly before I stomped to my front door. I opened it up and waited for her to walk through it. "You said what you had to say and I don't need to hear nothing else."

She laughed as she bent down and picked up her drink. She dropped the rest back and put the glass down on the table then walked up to the door. Instead of walking right out she stopped and turned toward me. With another long finger pointed in my face she said, "When my real best friend comes back to her senses, tell her to text me." She told me as she sauntered out the door and I slammed it behind her.

CHAPTER FOUR

TAE

I really wished I could have called out today and not gotten in trouble for it. I wasn't in the mood to be here and since I worked at a fried chicken fast food restaurant, where I was an assistant manager, it meant all I'm gonna get is trouble. But today, we were short staffed so I gotta be everybody. And it started with taking orders at the register.

"Welcome to *When You Can't We Chick-Can*, how can I serve you?" I asked a couple who stood in front of me.

"Ummm, let me get a 3 piece with an extra biscuit and what you want baby?" The guy asked the girl.

She looked at the sign over my head like she hadn't been here a million times already this week. "Can I have a grilled chicken salad with vinaigrette dressing and a diet coke." She looked at me.

He smiled at her and put his arm around her waist like she was really the one. They looked like they were so much in love. It's not too often you see public affection these days. They gotta be new. Puppy love. Bronco and me used to be just like them. Part of me wanted to pull her to the side and say, "Girl, don't let him pull you in no freak shit like my husband tried with me." But I decided to mind my own business.

"Ok, that'll be $11.11." I told them snapping out of my daydream.

The guy handed me his credit card and I swiped it. I gave him his receipt and card back. Before I took the next order, I removed my phone from my pocket to check and see if I had any texts or missed calls from Bronco.

I didn't.

My heart ached. Nobody told me this was how it would feel to be married. This shit sucked. When I blinked a few times I saw someone was standing in front of me. "Welcome to When You Can't We Chick-Can how may I—"

By KEESHIA K.

"Excuse me but I didn't get my cup for my drink." The lady I previously rang up interrupted me to say. "I been waiting here while you standing there looking all crazy and shit."

"Oh, I'm so sorry, ma'am." I said as I grabbed an extra large cup and handed it to her. I don't remember what size she paid for and I wasn't in the mood to check either. She snatched the cup, rolled her eyes and kept it moving.

I glanced up as she walked back over to her boyfriend. Now they were kissing and I wanted to throw up in my mouth. I missed my bae.

I decided to check and see if their food was ready because I had to get them out of my face or I might have had a panic attack.

When I looked behind me I saw their bag sitting under the heater. I grabbed it from the service window and walked it back to the counter. "Here you go." I handed the guy the bag. They didn't even say thank you. Just snatched it and left.

When I noticed another lady standing with tight folded arms I moved toward her. "I'm so sorry, ma'am. How can I serve you?"

"It's about time," she started. "I'll have a chicken salad sandwich meal—"

"Hey, my order's wrong." The guy with the girlfriend said cutting us off once again as he walked back up to the counter and looked through his bag.

"You know what, fuck this place," the woman who was interrupted said. "Ya'll chicken taste like some dust anyway." The frustrated woman walked out.

"You sure?" I asked, directing my attention to him.

"Yeah, my girl asked for grilled chicken salad and this is fried." He said.

"I told you that bitch was looking at you like she wanted you," his girlfriend whispered. "Can't even get our food order right."

I pretended like I didn't hear her even though she was right in my face. "Ok, I truly apologize. I must have heard you incorrectly. Give me one second to —"

"Hi, sir." My boss Carey interrupted me and said. "We will get that right to you. And we apologize for the mix up, we're a little short staffed but we appreciate your patience."

She must have overheard that his order was wrong. Fuck! Now I'm five seconds from losing my job.

"Taevonne, Ashley's gonna get them their food," Carey said. "Please come with me so we can talk a little." I followed her into the back office. Shit, I hate being reprimanded.

The moment we were alone she laid into me. "I know you aren't normally out front, but you used to be one of my best cashiers before your promotion." She told me as I listened and tried to keep my heart from thumping out of my chest. "But lately you've done nothing but ring in wrong orders. Not to mention that your drawer was short last night. What's going on with you?" She asked.

I swallowed the lump in my throat. "Carey, I'm just having some personal issues at home." I told her. I hoped my brief and general explanation would be enough.

"Well, I can understand that. But this is work and you're getting paid to do a job. Now, if you can't do it, I'll have to bring in someone who can. Are we clear?" She asked threatening my employment.

"Yes, I understand." I told her trying to hold back my tears. I needed to get myself together but didn't know how.

"Now take 5 minutes to get yourself in order back here then I need you on the floor." She told me before she walked out of the office.

I placed my face in my hands and took a deep breath. I can't function. I need to talk to Bronco. I need to know that our marriage isn't over. I need to know that he still wanted me. At this point I was willing to do or be anything he needed as long as he doesn't leave.

By KEESHIA K.

So I pulled out my phone to check it again. Still nothing. I looked at the clock on the office wall. Bronco should be on his break. Normally when he took it he would shoot me a text or forward me a funny meme. *I wonder if he's been on IG or Twitter?* I thought.

I opened up my Twitter app to see if he was active. He was. That hurt even more. Basically he had his phone in his hand but didn't use it to call me. He had to tell me something. I only had a couple more minutes before I needed to be back. I don't have time to wait to see if he texts me. "Fuck it." I said as I decided to call him.

I hit his number and when the call connected, it rang once then I was sent to his voicemail. He still had no words for me.

Wow.

I was blown, but I needed to fix this so I took another deep breath and when his voicemail finished and I heard the beep I started to speak. "Bronco, it's me, umm...I really need you to give me a call. I'm at work and I'm about to lose it not talking to you. Please, baby, let's put this back together. I miss you so much. Please call me." I hit end.

I was back on the floor and was relieved that the lunch rush was gone and it was slower than it had been before. After doing little jobs around the restaurant, I cleaned up the area near my register and when I finished, a woman walked up to it.

"Your collar is flipped up on the side." She told me as she reached over and put it down for me.

"Oh, thank you." I said blushing. She was taller than me, about 5'7, with naturally long sleek hair. Her nose was tiny but her eyes were wide and made her look innocent if it wasn't for her body. Plush lips. Big breasts. Tiny waist. All screaming come get me. I felt out of place in her presence so I ran my hand over my hair to make myself appear neater.

By KEESHIA K.

"No problem," she said with a huge smile. "I couldn't let someone as beautiful as you walk around like that." She continued.

"Aw, thank you. That's sweet of you to say." I told her smiling back. It was the first time I had genuinely smiled in days. She seemed to be staring at me longer than she should have. But, maybe I was over analyzing. She could just be nice.

"How can I serve you?" I asked her.

"That's what she said." She told me.

I burst out laughing. "I love that show." I said acknowledging that I got her joke from *The Office*.

She giggled. "I'm sorry, I couldn't resist. I love it too." She stated as she looked over my head at the menu. For some reason I wanted her to take her time so I can really look at her. But why?

I cleared my throat. "See anything you want yet?" I asked still smiling.

She looked directly into my eyes. "For now I'll take a number 3."

She winked, reached into her purse and pulled out her credit card. When she handed it to me I caught a whiff of her perfume. Not only was she gorgeous, she smelled amazing. She looked like the type of woman Bronco would be attracted to.

Then it hit me. I knew just how I was gonna get my husband back. He laid out to me what he wanted before we were married. Now I either had to play the game or lose him forever. I just hoped she was willing to assist.

"You look like you're into having a good time," I started handing her back her credit card. "Would you like to hang out later?" I asked throwing all caution to the wind. It seemed like an eternity passed while I awaited her answer.

She smiled and said, "My calendar is wide open, what you got in mind?"

By KEESHIA K.

CHAPTER FIVE
BRONCO

I pushed down 295 on my way home. It was a warm night so I had my roof open and my windows down as I blasted *'Kevin's Heart.'* by J. Cole. I just finished working overtime at the dealership where I was a mechanic and relieved to finally be off.

All I wanted to do was take a hot shower, throw the Redskins and Giants game on and grab some grub. I ain't feel like arguing tonight with the wife but I had a feeling it may be unavoidable. Ever since Tae left me that message I knew the days of us walking around the house in silence were over. She was going to do all she could to get me to talk to her, even though I wanted to avoid it.

'Aight...I mean, I know it was wrong for me to be getting head out Mexico, but shit, shawty came on to me hard. She wasn't no dime or nothing like Tae but she just kept talking 'bout how *long and strong* my hands were and she wondered what I was packing.

By KEESHIA K.

Shit, I had to give her this dick. What else was I 'sposed to do?

What Tae gotta realize is she the wife. She the one that got my heart as long as she don't renege on a nigga. I know technically what I did wasn't in my rules to pull Tae in before I stepped out but give a nigga a break. I was out the country and we just got married. It would take some time for me to break old habits.

I pressed on the brake as the evening traffic was at a momentary standstill. I used the pause to light my Capone. As I pulled on it, I looked over into the car on my left. An older woman was behind the wheel and when she looked over at me, she rolled her eyes and looked back out in front of her. The fuck I do to her?

I licked my lips and chuckled before turning my music louder and blowing the smoke out the window. My sounds were interrupted by an incoming call. When I looked at the screen I saw it was Tae.

Damn, she couldn't even give me peace on my drive home. Fuck it. I decided to take the call. I mean we was gonna get into this eventually anyway. Plus, if I'm being honest, I jive missed her.

Since my phone was paired to my truck's sound system through Bluetooth, I hit the button on my dash to connect to the call. "Yeah, hello," I said out loud before pressing the gas since I was now able to drive forward. I took a deep pull from my Capone.

"Hey, Bronc. Look, baby, I know you had a long day, so I made dinner, turkey meatloaf, garlic mashed potatoes, broccoli and blueberry muffins." She told me. "Were you planning on coming home to eat?"

She did that shit on purpose. She knew it was real hard for me to resist that meal. Especially after I worked OT. "Yeah, I guess." I said dryly, grabbing my dick. I had to piss like a horse. I hated when I didn't go before I left work. I knew traffic could be a bitch but mechanics are the nastiest group of niggas you ever could imagine. I couldn't stand pissing in that bathroom.

"Great!" She said excitedly.

"But look, I ain't up for a whole lot of arguing, Tae." I made it clear. "I mean it ain't fair that I laid the shit out for you before we got married and you still ain't getting with the program. I'ma need a steady stream of bitches like some niggas need a steady stream of income."

"Bronco, I get it now. I do. I know what I signed up for and I'm ready to be the wife you need me to be." She told me.

I smiled. I do miss her. Especially how sexy she looked when she bounced on my pole. My wife was perfect. She had honey brown skin with freckles on her nose, big soft titties and a plump ass that went on for days. I can't wait to slide in that tonight now that I think about it. "Aight, well, I'm in traffic, be there soon." I said before ending the call.

I took another pull from my Capone and looked out at the cars ahead of me. When I realized it was more than I could wait through before pissing on myself, I jumped over into the right lane after the car on the side of me hesitated. I took the exit and was right by my parent's house. I decided to go use their bathroom.

When I pulled up, I saw my dad's car in the driveway but my mom's car wasn't there. I figured she was working the night shift and he was home probably watching the game.

After I parked, I gripped at my dick again to try and control my bladder. At this point I really had to go now. It seemed like the closer I was to pissing the worse the urge was. I felt like I was gonna explode.

I hopped out my truck and dashed up the walkway. I reached down behind the hose rack and grabbed the spare key. When I put it in and unlocked the door, I was halted entry by the chain. "What the fuck?" I said as I peeped through the crack looking for my father.

KNOCK! KNOCK! KNOCK! "Pop! It's me, open up." I yelled into the house. The hallway light came on and my father came into my line of sight.

By KEESHIA K.

"What you doing here, man?" My pop asked as he finally approached the door. He still hadn't opened it.

"I was on my way home but traffic a monster and I gotta pee bad." I explained to him wondering why I still stood on the porch jumping from foot to foot, as I tried to prevent myself from wetting up everything out there.

"Aw, man, do like I do and piss in the bushes 'round back." He instructed before he turned around and started walking away.

"Come on, pop. You know I can't pee in public. It's just gonna hurt and not come out because I'ma be worried that somebody looking at me. Let me in, man, please." I pleaded with him.

He shook his head, looked behind him and then turned back around to face me. He pushed the door closed with an attitude and I heard the chain slide through the latch. Finally he snatched it back open and stood back.

I busted through the doorway like I had a search warrant. "Thanks, pop. I won't be — ", my sentence was cut short when I glanced past the bathroom and saw a gray haired woman, who wasn't my moms, with watermelons for titties adjusting the buttons on her white blouse sitting on the couch.

I turned around and looked at my father. "What's going on, man?" I asked stunned.

He cut his eyes to where the woman was and then walked up to me close. I guess so she couldn't hear what he was gonna say next. "Look here, she's a friend of mine I know from work. She stopped by to bring me some papers I needed to sign and we were just talking is all." My father told me.

A friend. Fuck I look like old man...A newbie? I thought. "So Ma knows she's here?" I asked not buying his bullshit.

"Boy, your mother ain't my mother!" He said in a strong whisper. "I ain't got to clear shit with her 'fore I do anything." He pointed a stiff finger into my chest. "This my house."

I was heated, but I still had to piss. So, without another word, I turned away from him and walked into the bathroom.

I was so hot when I got inside I almost put my fist through the back of the door. I couldn't believe this nigga was fucking another woman in this house. I mean, it was no secret that my father used to have women on the side from time to time. Shit, when I was little, he would take me along with him when he did his thing, but I had never known him to bring no bitch home where my mother lived too. That's just dirty.

"Fuck this dude." I said out loud as I unzipped my coveralls and let my pee stream into my father's Timbs. He left his smelly boots in the downstairs bathroom occasionally and today they would play host to my angry urine. "If he wanna disrespect, so will I."

CHAPTER SIX
BRONCO

I was still mad AF when I made it home. My father called and went off 'bout his boots, but I ain't give a fuck. Maybe he'll reflect on how foul that shit was while he out buying new ones.

When I walked through my apartment door, I was shocked not only to see Tae sitting on the couch looking like a snack, but another dime sitting with her. I'd never seen her before and I immediately felt my hormones about to shift into fast track mode. Please, God prevent me from fucking her new friend.

"Hey, bae!" Tae said excitedly. "I'm so glad you're home." She hopped off the couch and approached me with a wine glass in her hand. I could see that her eyes were glassy and knew she was buzzed.

"What's good?" I said before I cut my eyes to our guest who was also holding a glass of red wine.

"This is Siena. She's a friend, well, a new friend who has agreed to join us for dinner." She told me as she took my duffle bag from me. "I hope you don't mind."

Join us for dinner? I thought. Could she mean shawty was down to fuck? Oh man, my wife is the real MVP if she pulled this off. Damn! What a beautiful thing to come home to I swear for gawd!

"How you doing, Siena." I said making my way over to the couch for a closer look. "I'm Bronco, I would shake your hand but I been working on cars all day and should scrub 'em first."

"That's ok," she said as she stood up. "Tae has told me so much about you I feel like I already know you."

"Oh, is that right?" I asked looking at my wife who had the biggest smile on her face. I licked my lips. "All good things I hope." I laughed as I willed my dick to stay down just thinking about all the nasty shit I had planned for them. "Well look, let me grab a shower and I be right back. But you stay right there." I winked at Tae and headed to the bathroom.

"Anymore wine, Tae?" I asked stopping in my tracks. I turned back around and stole another look. I needed to catch up to where they were.

"Oh, yes. Let me get it for you." She paused and focused on her friend. "Excuse me for a second, Siena." She made her way to the kitchen. Siena sat back down and sipped her wine.

"Here you go." Tae said handing me a full bottle of Riesling. I took it from her and smiled. She leaned forward, and stood on her tiptoes for a kiss. I bent down to give her a big one. "Still mad at me?"

"You got my head fucked up with this sexy shit right here," I said. I kissed her and her lips were soft and wet and tasted like wine. She licked my bottom lip and sucked it hard before pulling away. Now my shit was rock hard. She looked down at it and licked her lips. I pulled the cork on the wine, took a huge gulp and smacked her ass before I turned around and walked away taking the bottle with me.

I beat my dick in the shower before washing up. I had to get that first nut out because the last thing I needed was to bust off too fast when I had serious work to put in for the night.

When I walked back out into the living room, I noticed how close Siena and Tae were sitting to each other. They both had low eyes and were giggling and falling all over each other. I downed over half of the wine that I had left and walked closer to them.

"Bronco, you want me to make your plate." Tae asked getting up and approaching me.

"Naw, I'll eat it later." I told her. "Ya'll look cozy though. Got a spot on the couch for me?" I asked before I licked my lips.

"Absolutely," Tae said grabbing my hand. We walked over to the couch and I sat down. I elected to put some casual gear on so they didn't have to waste too much time undressing me. I had on my wife beater and basketball shorts. No draws.

Tae sat on my right and Siena was on my left and I knew what time it was but I wanted to make sure they did too before I jumped out there. "So, what ya'll feel like doing?" I asked getting right into it. I looked at Tae and noticed how her chest moved up and down like it did in the past right before she had a panic attack. "Bae, you aight?" I asked feeling my anger rising. If she fucked this shit up by passing out I'ma be hot.

"Yeah, I'm good. Just a little nervous." Tae said taking a deep breath. "I'll be ok." She grabbed the bottle of water sitting on the table and took a gulp. I put the wine bottle down and got up to go grab her a cool rag. When I came back I placed it on her neck.

"It's aight, baby," I said as softly as I could without snapping. "Relax." I hoped how nice I sounded would be enough to calm her nerves.

"Taevonne, look around." Siena told her. She did. "It's just you, me and your husband. There's no

By KEESHIA K.

audience. No one to judge. Just relax and do what comes natural." She continued.

Damn, Siena was good. When I looked at Tae her chest was no longer moving up and down. She smiled at Siena then at me. Since Tae had candles lit throughout the living room, I walked over to the light switch and flipped it off. Trying to do my portion to set the mood.

I walked back to the couch and sat between them. When I looked over at Tae and leaned in for a kiss, she kissed me back, deeply. Suddenly I felt a hand on my left thigh. It was Siena's. I continued kissing my wife but reached over with my left hand and put it on Siena's thigh.

Siena leaned in and kissed my neck and for the second time within twenty minutes, my dick got rock hard. I slid my hand up Siena's thigh slowly and her skin was soft but firm. I could tell she worked out. Ready to set this shit off, I took my right hand and grabbed Tae's breast. Her nipples were hard. *Yes!* I thought. It meant she was turned on.

Wanting to be an equal opportunity type of nigga, I stopped kissing Tae and turned my attention towards Siena. She sat up and then leaned in for a kiss from me. I put my wet lips on hers and was impressed. They were plump and soft and I wanted to devour them.

I didn't feel anything happening on my right side and wondered what Tae was doing. To make sure she wasn't about to make me fuck her up by not playing along, I stopped kissing Siena and looked over at Tae. Her eyes were low, but not in an angry way. I was in the clear. This look was the one she gave when she was ready to fuck.

Playing director, I sat deeper back into the couch and pushed Siena and Tae into each other slowly. Letting them know I wanted them to kiss. They moved toward one another until their lips met. I watched them kiss passionately and had to shift my dick a little before I stabbed everybody. It was so hard now it hurt.

After some time, Tae stopped kissing Siena and looked at me. I licked my lips and said, "Get them clothes off." She immediately followed my order and started undressing. I looked at Siena. "You too." She

66   *By KEESHIA K.*

followed my command and started to strip. Now it was time for the next level so I slid my shorts and wife beater off.

Tae wasted no time on me. She gripped my dick and shoved it between her lips. Her mouth felt so hot and wet, I immediately started to pump into her. Siena reached down with her left hand and juggled my balls while leaning into me for another kiss. My lips met hers again and our tongues danced inside each other's mouths while my wife took care of the heavy equipment. When she was really sucking that shit, I put my hand on the back of Tae's head to keep her right where she was.

I couldn't believe this was really happening. It felt so fucking good and was better than my wildest dreams. Shit, it felt a little too good to be true. I stopped kissing Siena and pulled Tae's hair to stop her from deep throating me. I couldn't shoot my load before sampling the new pussy.

Feeling like the world was mine I got up off the couch. "Siena, lay down." I told her. When she did. I got in between her legs and slid inside her. *Oh my fucking God.* I thought. She was so wet and tight I couldn't believe it. I loved it. It made me feel like she wasn't run through. I slow stroked her while winding my hips to make sure I hit all her spots.

She put her hand on my chest and circled my nipple with her index finger. "Fuck, you feel good." I told her. She looked over at Tae who was watching us fuck like we were a movie.

"Come here," Siena told Tae. She crawled over to Siena but looked unsure of what to do. "Climb up on my face." She instructed Tae.

Tae stood up on the side of the couch and swung her legs over, positioning her pussy right over Siena's mouth. Siena gripped Tae's thighs and went to work. She licked and sucked all over Tae's pussy. I could see her cream oozing out onto Siena's chin.

"Mmmmmmmmmmmm," Tae moaned as she rocked her hips back and forth. I felt my nut creeping up on me as I watched the show and wanted to cum hard. So I opened Siena's legs wider and leaned into her, pumping in and out with force.

See most niggas need to be like me. Let these bitches know up front what they want. Why be a one-woman man when you could have plenty? My life can get nothing but better from here. That's for sure.

"Ahhh, Ahhhh, Ahhh," was all Siena could say with pussy in her mouth while I fucked her brains out. When I saw Tae grab her own nipples and squeeze I knew she was about to cum too. I gave Siena two more pumps and then pulled my dick out and shot my load on her stomach.

"MMMMMMaaaaaaahhhhhhhhhh," Tae screamed out as her body convulsed.

If this was any example of how good my life was gonna be, I was with this shit. I breathed heavily trying to catch my breath and looked at Tae just as she turned around to look at me. *We did it.* I thought. I was so proud of my bae. Now, finally, this looked like the start of a beautiful marriage.

CHAPTER SEVEN

TAE

When I woke up, I rolled over and tapped my cell phone that sat on the table near my side of the bed. I received a text message about a sale at *Nasty Gal's* clothing and I sighed. When I saw that it was eight o'clock in the morning, I rolled back over and stretched out for Bronco. He was still knocked out from our ongoing fuck fest.

Last night, and early this morning if I'm being honest, was insane. I have never experienced multiple orgasms before in my life. They were non-stop. It was something to be said for making a decision to jump out there and then dive in headfirst. And as long as Bronco was happy, what was the harm?

Yawning, I sat up and looked on the other side of Bronco for Siena. She wasn't in the bed. The bathroom light was off so I assumed she wasn't in there either. Maybe she left. I was on my way to get up and check when I smelled coffee.

By KEESHIA K.

I smiled at the thought that Siena may have been nice enough to put on a pot. I didn't want to disturb Bronco so I grabbed my blue silk robe off the back of the door and crept out of our bedroom.

When I got to the kitchen I saw Siena in front of the stove scrambling eggs. Not only did she make coffee but she made breakfast too. I leaned against the wall and took the scene in. It was very erotic.

I couldn't get over how sexy Siena looked in only Bronco's white wife beater. The bottom of it barely covered her ass cheeks and she had her hair pulled up into a messy bun on top of her head. I thought about all the things we did last night and a chill ran through my body.

Pulling myself together I shook my head and peeled myself off the wall. "Good morning." I said as I walked into the kitchen.

"Oh, no you're awake." She pouted. She looked upset. "You're not supposed to be up yet. I wanted to bring you both breakfast in bed." She said seductively.

"Aw, that's so sweet." A smile spread across my face. "Well, Bronco's still sleep. How about I leave you to it and go jump back in bed?" I suggested.

"Great!" She said excitedly as she clapped her hands. "I'll be there in about five minutes." She told me.

I turned around and dashed back up the hallway and back into my bedroom. I crept as soon as I walked through the door to be as quiet as possible and not disturb my husband. But when I looked over at him I saw that he was already up.

"Oh, morning, baby." I removed my robe and tossed it on the foot of the bed. "What you doing?" I asked playfully before climbing back into bed and straddling him.

"What's up, Mrs. Lawson?" He said as he grabbed my hips and pumped his morning hard on into the seat of my thong. "Sleep good?"

"I slept like a baby." I told him before I bent down and kissed his lips. "But I'm surprised you still poking me down there. You ain't drained from our wild sex-ca-pade?" I joked.

"Hell no! You know I'm never satisfied." He said before he smacked me on my ass cheek. It stung but made my clit jump.

"Where Siena?" He looked behind me. "She bounced already?" He asked before he put both his hands behind his head and stretched.

"No, she's out in the kitchen cooking us breakfast." I grinned. "From what I saw she has eggs, turkey bacon, hash browns, toast and coffee." I informed him.

"Damn, mean in the sack and she cook too." He yawned. "Oh well, it's gonna be hard saying goodbye to her."

My eyes widened. "Goodbye…Why would we say goodbye? I thought you wanted a situation like this. I mean, weren't you pleased with her?" I asked confused at what he really wanted.

"It ain't that, Tae. Remember, I said variety. That means different women, no permanents." He told me. "Keeping a woman around in a situation like ours can get too messy." He informed me. "She'd just get in the way."

I was disappointed. I really liked Siena and more importantly I was comfortable with her. She was very attentive to him and me. "Ok, Bronco. You know best." I looked down into his eyes.

"That's why you married me." He winked at me and pulled me down onto him. We kissed passionately as he began to grind his pelvis against mine.

Outside The Bedroom Door

Siena stood on the other side of the bedroom door slouched down with her ear pressed against it. In her hands,

By KEESHIA K.

she held a tray that contained the breakfast she made for the couple.

But before she went inside the room, she overheard the conversation that Bronco and Tae had about her not being a permanent fixture in their marriage and she was disappointed. She thought they all had a good time the night before and now she was certain that what they shared was over. Not being one to take rejection well, Siena decided to do the slicing before she got sliced.

Taking a deep breath, she stood up straight and put a smile on her face. She turned around and proceeded through the door using her butt to push it open. "Good morning you two." She said as she pivoted around and walked over to the end of the bed. "It's breakfast time!"

She was shocked to see Tae on top of Bronco in a heated petting session and grinned harder. "Wow, I guess if I would have been five minutes more in the kitchen this scene would be a lot different." She said playfully.

Tae wiped her lips and rolled off Bronco, sitting up in bed yoga style. Yeah, sorry we kind of got carried away." Tae laughed.

Bronco sat up and positioned himself to take the tray from Siena. "No apologies necessary. Ya'll newlyweds, you supposed to be on top of each other, always." Siena joked. "Well, here is your breakfast and coffee. I wasn't sure how you drank it so I brought in cream and sugar." She told them.

"Damn, this looks good." Bronco said eyeing the tray. "Thanks, ma." He told her as he winked and grabbed a slice of turkey bacon.

"It sure does, Siena. And I'm so hungry." Tae said as she reached across Bronco and grabbed a cup of coffee.

"No thanks needed." She paused. "It was my pleasure." Siena exhaled. "Listen, I'm gonna go ahead and cut out now." She continued. "You both should be good right?"

He frowned. "Wait, you not gonna eat first?" Bronco asked, a mouth full of eggs and hash browns.

"No, I been here long enough." Siena informed. "Last night was fun, but it's morning and that means back to reality." She continued.

76   *By KEESHIA K.*

Tae looked at Bronco.

"Just let me slip into the bathroom and get dressed and I'll leave you to it," Siena continued. She smiled and grabbed her clothes that were folded on the chair. Walking into the bathroom she closed the door behind herself.

15 Minutes Later

Bronco

Damn, shawty was cool. Normally you gotta kick the third wheel out in the morning before shit got awkward. I thought. "You know, maybe Siena won't be too bad to bring back again." I told Tae before I took a sip of my coffee. "I like the fact that she ain't wanna intrude on the marriage and dipped. That was classy."

"I thought so, too. I mean, if we gonna do this, Bronco, I really like her for us. I think she can be a good addition." She said. "At least until I'm more comfortable and we can figure this thing out."

"Aight cool, it's settled. She got the green light to come back." I said as I nodded my head and licked my lips.

CHAPTER EIGHT

TAE

I was extremely nervous. Tonight, Bronco's and my parents were coming over for dinner. This was an event that has never happened before. I mean, they were all together at our wedding of course, but never alone with just Bronco and me and since Bronco's father was somewhat of a loose cannon and was liable to say and do anything, I didn't know what to expect.

What also had me so shook is that our parents are the complete opposites of each other. And the only thing they have in common is that their children married one another. Who some people may say are also the opposite of each other, considering everything that had been happening lately.

This may not end too well. I thought.

"Damn, baby, what smells so fire?" Bronco said walking through the door. He just got in from work and I was relieved he was on time. Earlier he told me he may have to stay late but he wanted me to still cook for our parents if he did. What I wasn't interested in doing was having to entertain both of our parents alone.

"I'm so glad you here," I told him as I put down the spoon I stirred the pasta with and ran into his open arms. "I don't think I would have been able to do this without you."

"What you mean?" He asked wrapping his arms around my waist. "They just our folks, bae."

"I know, and I love my parents, you know I do but they tend to overdue it in the affection department. I just hope they don't make your mom and dad feel weird." I lied.

The truth was I never knew what was liable to come out of Bronco's father's mouth. He could be so rude at times it was gross. Not just to strangers but mainly to his own wife.

"Tae, don't trip, baby. It's gonna be all good. Your folks ain't fixing to start fucking on the dining room

By KEESHIA K.

table or nothing, are they?" Bronco asked me. "I mean they can contain themselves long enough for a meal right?"

"Of course not," I laughed, hitting his arm. "Don't be stupid."

"Then we straight." He said smacking my ass. "I'ma go grab a shower right fast. They'll be here shortly."

"Ok." I said turning away from him. I walked back to the stove. I know he said we were good but something told me I should start drinking now. I don't care what Bronco says; I think someone may get their feelings hurt tonight. As a matter of fact I was sure of it.

"Baby, this shrimp pasta is amazing." My father said to me across the dinner table. "Is this a new recipe?" He asked. "If so you have to share it with your mother."

"Yep, daddy. I normally make it with spicy turkey sausage. But since everyone doesn't eat meat I threw in the shrimp instead." I explained. "I'm glad you like it though."

We all sat at the table eating and just like I thought; something was going on between Bronco and Mr. Lawson. He never told me that him and his father had some sort of beef, so I was curious to find out what was up. The way he treated him made everybody uncomfortable.

"It's aight, a little too fishy for me," Mr. Lawson said. "I would have preferred to have the sausage if I'm being totally honest." He shrugged. "But to each his own."

"Well, pop. You ain't gotta eat nothing you don't want to. I promise, our feelings won't be hurt." Bronco

By KEESHIA K.

replied defending my dinner. "You ain't got to eat ever again if you really feeling that way."

Mr. Lawson sucked food out of his teeth and after making the sucking noise for what seemed like forever he used his extra long pinky fingernail to dig in between them. He finally got the food out but then he sucked it back into his mouth from under his nail and started chewing it. He was so disgusting.

"I think it tastes very good, Taevonne," Bronco's mother said to me. "You must share this recipe. Maybe I can try my hand at it later. I mean, it won't be as good as yours but I'll try."

"Please don't, Taevonne." Mr. Lawson said referring to Bronco's mother, his own wife. "She don't need to be cooking no more pasta." He looked over at her. "She done got fat enough as is. What you need to find are some good salad recipes. If you spread across the bed any wider, you may be sleeping on the floor because I'm not fucking with you." He continued while he stabbed at his dinner.

"Pop!" Bronco yelled out.

I looked away from Mrs. Lawson. I was too embarrassed to keep eye contact with her. Instead I cut my eyes over towards my mother. She was chewing her pasta while she side eyed my dad.

"Pop what?" Mr. Lawson asked Bronco. "You know I ain't lying. And that outfit she got on tonight don't do nothing but make it worse." He paused. "I mean look at her."

"Come on, Phil. Don't you think you being a little harsh, man?" My father said to Bronco's father. Oh shit, the drama has started and we didn't even get a chance to have dessert.

"Say, brother, this here is my wife. I can talk about her any way I damn well please. Don't you worry 'bout how *harsh* you think I am." Mr. Lawson continued. "Ain't nobody talking to you no way."

I looked at my father with pleading eyes not to say anything else. I didn't want this situation to get more out of hand than it already was. I knew this night would be a bust.

By KEESHIA K.

My father looked at my mother and then at me. He winked and nodded his head. "You absolutely right, Phil. That is your wife...*why* she's your wife I'm sure I don't know." My father continued. "But still she is."

Mr. Lawson put his fork down and his nose flared while he stared at my father. "Ain't none of your motherfucking business why she my wife, brother." He yelled across the table with food flying out of his mouth. "Now you making me think you feeling some way about her."

My father put his fork down now and looked at Mr. Lawson. But before he could shoot back, my mother put her hand on his knee. He looked at her and took a deep breath. Then he wiped his mouth with his napkin and took a sip from his wine glass.

Mrs. Lawson kept her head down in her plate. She hadn't looked up once since her husband unleashed on her.

Bronco shook his head and downed his beer not saying a word. Mr. Lawson continued to suck food out of his teeth while he looked at my father and smirked.

I felt a headache starting to form in the front of my head and took a large gulp of wine from my glass.

We all ate the rest of the meal in silence.

Dinner was over, Thank God and our parents were about to leave. I was in the kitchen loading the dishwasher when my father approached me. "Baby, thank you again for inviting us over for that great meal. Your mother and I really appreciated it." He said grabbing me into a warm hug.

"No problem, daddy." I kissed his cheek. "I'm sorry about Mr. Lawson, but thank you for not escalating the situation more." I sighed. "It was so hard to watch."

"Baby, don't apologize for a grown man. That's not on you. But I do want you to think about something." He told me as he stared into my eyes. "You need to be careful about Bronco. A man is a reflection of his parents. And a son is a copy of his father. What you witnessed tonight may be in your near future if you aren't careful." He finished and kissed me on the forehead.

When he walked out my kitchen I immediately thought about how Bronco made me bring a woman into our marriage. Could this be the start of him turning into Mr. Lawson? *I hope for my sake that my daddy gets this one wrong.* To be honest I'm praying it's not the case.

CHAPTER NINE
BRONCO

"Let me get that for you, beautiful." I told my wife as we approached *Club Deuce*. "Looking as sexy as you are you shouldn't have to open your own door." I licked my lips and winked.

I told Tae I wanted to take her out on a date to celebrate being Mr. and Mrs. and she was so sised and couldn't wait to step out with a nigga. But truth be told, it had been a week since our little threesome and I needed more of that. If I played my cards right tonight we could have a lot of fun.

"Thank you, husband." Tae said to me walking through the door wearing my favorite dress. Whenever she put it on, I knew she wanted to have a long night of fucking. Little did she know that was exactly what I had in store for us.

When we got inside, I slipped the bouncer a hundo for VIP seating. He put us in a nice spot too with the

By KEESHIA K.

perfect view. Not too far from the dance floor and the bar.

"This is so nice, Bronco." She looked around the small piece of real estate we owned for the night. "Thank you for taking me out and showing me a good time." She smiled. "I'm excited."

"I love seeing you smile. You know that?" I asked Tae getting her right where I wanted her. She cheesed harder. "It lets me know everything gonna be good with us."

"I love seeing you smile too, baby." She said before taking a sip of champagne.

"You do huh?" I asked. "Well, being honest, I haven't really smiled since we had our first threesome. And if you really want to know, I'm ready to smile again." I told her. "Understand what I'm saying?"

"Oh...Ok, do you want me to contact Siena and have her come join us again?" Tae asked me. "I'm sure she wouldn't mind. She had a lot of fun with us the last time and —"

"Naw, I mean I know we said we'd let her come through again but not yet." I touched the side of her face. "I wanna try something new out now." I looked out into the club. "See what else lands."

She was quiet. Her eyes rolled over me and then down into the drink that sat between her hands. "Oh, that's what you mean." She sighed "I...I don't know if—"

"Listen, I'm right here with you. All I wanna do is watch you come on to about three broads. As sexy as you are you should be able to get a least one to come home with us tonight." I told her as I licked my lips and took a swig of champagne. "I mean look at you."

"You want me to come...on...to...three women?" She looked around the club. "In here...tonight?" She asked surprised. "Bronco, this ain't even a gay club. What if I make a fool of myself?"

"But what if you don't?" I said to her.

"But...How? I don't know what to do." She asked me looking like she was on the verge of tears. "I...I barely knew what to do with Siena."

"It ain't that hard, bae. When you see a chick that you know I would like, just do what you did to get Siena to come home with you." I reminded her. "That was first round draft pick work you put in there, I don't mind telling you. Just do it again."

She looked over at the bar and I followed her eyes and glanced where she was looking. At the moment there were two women who were sitting and drinking. A brown skin baddie and a redbone.

I caught Tae's eye and nodded in the direction of the brown skin chick. "Go get her." I coached. "Start there."

Tae let out a deep breath and gulped down the remainder of her drink. Then she grabbed the bottle and filled her glass back up. When she was ready she stood up and walked away from our table.

AT THE BAR

TAE

I cannot believe I was getting ready to approach this woman and try to convince her to come home with my husband and me. I tried to remain as calm as possible and not have a panic attack but I felt light on my feet. Almost like I was floating and about to pass out.

Still I agreed to do this so I had to at least try. I took a deep breath and walked up next to where the woman sat and put my drink down on the bar. "Excuse me," I started. "H-How you doing tonight?" I stuttered.

"I'm good." She said with an attitude. I cut my eyes across the way to Bronco who was staring daggers at me. I sighed and turned my attention back to the woman. "This is a nice club. It's my first time here. You ever been—"

By KEESHIA K.

"Look, I don't know if you know, but this here is a straight club and I ain't with no dyke shit! Now get the fuck up out my face." She shouted before she swiveled around on her stool.

I was humiliated. I started to go back to the table where Bronco was but as I headed back, he stood up and pointed toward the bar. I stopped walking and looked at him. I opened my hands and shrugged my shoulders trying to let him know it didn't work. He didn't care. He shook his head and pointed harder.

I took another sigh in defeat. I pivoted back around with my head down and walked to a different part of the bar. There were a few more women on this side and I saw a couple that I figured Bronco would be attracted to.

I decided to try a different approach this time.

"What you drinking?" I asked the random woman I walked up to. She looked me up and down and busted out laughing. I turned my head to see if someone was behind me. There wasn't, she was definitely laughing at me. She shook her head and continued dancing in her seat as if I wasn't even standing there.

Shamed and embarrassed again, I turned around and caught the eye of another attractive woman ordering a drink from the bar tender. When I got up enough nerve, which seemed like forever, I walked over and stood next to her. She looked over at me and grinned. Relieved she was probably nice, I grinned back. "You have a beautiful smile." I told her.

"Um, thank you." She replied and looked over at the bar tender who was making her drink.

"Would you like to get out of here?" I asked deciding to skip the pleasantries since they seemed not to work anyway. Plus I felt like it was just a matter of time before word got out that some lesbian was running around the club stalking women.

"With who...you?" She asked. I nodded. Her smile disappeared and she looked like I spit in her face. "Bitch, I don't do fish! I'm all about that beef and if you

By KEESHIA K.

don't get the fuck out my face I'm gonna cut that pussy licking tongue out your mouth!" She yelled.

I took off running.

THE BATHROOM
TAE

I was in the bathroom stall crying my eyes out. Not only had three different women humiliated me, but also it was my husband who set me up for this embarrassment. I don't know if I'm gonna be able to handle this situation with him wanting to be with other women. I mean, why couldn't we just keep Siena?

When I got myself together and walked out of the stall I was shocked to see a woman standing in front of it looking at me. She must have walked in when I was balling which would explain why I didn't hear her. But

I know she heard me. Great! Now I'm more embarrassed.

"Are you ok?" The stranger asked. "I heard you crying when I walked in. I was waiting for you to come out to make sure everything was alright. And to see if there was anything I could do."

"Thank you. I think I'll be fine. I just need to figure some things out that's all." I told her. I turned the water on and grabbed a paper towel to clean up my face. My make up was ruined.

"Well, I'm not sure what's going on, but I hate to see beautiful women crying." She said. "And I know you don't know me, but if there's anything I can do to help, I will." She touched my shoulder.

My eyebrows rose and I stared at her in the mirror, finally paying attention to what she looked like. She wasn't a complete dime but she was cute, put together well and smelled good. More importantly, she was attentive to me. Which at this point was the biggest part of it all. I needed attention and it was obvious my husband wasn't with giving me any.

By KEESHIA K.

I turned off the water, took a deep breath and moved toward her. "Maybe there is something you can do for me after all."

CHAPTER TEN
BRONCO

That shit worked! I knew if I put the press on Tae my night would end up lit just like this...knee deep in *new* pussy. The shawty that Tae brought back to the table wasn't no knock out but I ain't fucking her face. Well, maybe just a little bit. Still, she was definitely doable and for that I give my wife thumbs up.

"That's right, shawty, I wanna feel your tonsils." I said while she had my dick in her mouth. Her head game was ok, but I know she can be great if I applied a little more pressure. So I gripped the back of her neck and shoved my shit deeper into her mouth.

She stood up on her knees and took in my whole shaft and I was impressed. "Yeah, that's it." I coached as I threw my head back and closed my eyes. I realized that all this action with shawty was good but I didn't feel nothing else. Where was my support team? Where was Tae?

By KEESHIA K.

When I opened my eyes and looked around the room Tae was sitting on the side of the bed looking lost. She definitely wasn't doing all that she was on our first time out. "Bae, what you doing?" I asked, while I tried not to get annoyed. "Jump in here." I told her.

She rolled over near us and started to kiss me. I kissed her back, but it was dry. Like she'd rather be sleep or something. When she pulled away from me and looked down at our guest I knew something was off with her. Shawty was putting in serious work.

Tae scooted her body down to try and get some of this dick action but the chick ain't make room. I could tell she was a solo type of bitch. Maybe the wife didn't like that sort of thing. So Tae maneuvered her body around to try and fondle my balls.

Shawty finally noticed her and sat up. She reached over and kissed Tae while jerking my dick. But after only what seemed like thirty seconds she stopped kissing Tae.

"Put this pipe in me, big daddy!" She told me. I grabbed at her waist and positioned her on top of me. I gave her the full 'D'. "Ohhhhhh…" She moaned loudly while squeezing her nipples and winding her hips. "That feel so, so right. Please don't stop."

Tae bent in and tried to kiss her again but the chick threw her head back instead ignoring her. Tae tried again by getting up and going to her other side. She leaned over and attempted to kiss her but this time shawty moved down and kissed me instead.

I don't know what was up with her but her and Tae were out of sync. No connection at all. Maybe Tae wasn't drunk enough and was too uptight so the girl may be feeling that. The last time we did this Tae and Siena had been drinking before I even got home. So maybe she just needed to get some liquid courage.

I stopped kissing the chick and looked at Tae. "Bae, go grab us some wine. I think you could use some to loosen up a bit." I was still pumping into shawty and to be honest I didn't really give a fuck if she did or didn't loosen up just as long as she ain't fuck my shit

By KEESHIA K.

up with the bird. 'Cuz for real I'm just focusing on busting this nut. Nothing less. Nothing more.

"Ok, baby." Tae said getting up off the bed. As she grabbed her robe and headed toward the door, I flipped shawty over and started hitting her from the back.

IN THE LIVING ROOM
TAE

Bronco thought that me drinking would loosen me up but I'm not the only one that's not trying. That bitch doesn't want me there at all. This whole situation is crazy but I know if I don't go along I could lose my husband. It was like a cloud was over my head the entire time.

It's not like I was totally opposed to the whole ordeal anyway. I mean when we first did it with Siena, we had a good time. Not only was Siena and I compatible but it brought Bronco and I closer together. Or so I thought. But now I feel wrong.

I really don't understand why we needed to bring in new women. Siena would be perfect to mix it up every once in a while. I really wished Bronco saw it that way too.

I looked at the door and my mind thought about the past. I wonder what Siena's doing. Maybe I should call her and see if she would be interested in coming back over and being with us again. I might as well, ain't like I'm missed in the bedroom right now anyway.

I grabbed my cell phone that was on the dining room table. I searched through my contacts until I found her number. I never put it in my phone because she actually did it herself and when I saw her name, I smiled. She added a heart emoji next to her number.

By KEESHIA K.

Before I hit the telephone symbol to call her, I decided to pour myself a glass of wine. I wanted to be relaxed because right now I felt confused and uptight. When I walked to the kitchen and heard smacking sounds and moaning coming from my bedroom my stomach churned. They sounded like they were still going hard.

After I got my drink I walked over to the couch and made the call. I was nervous and crossed my fingers that she picked up.

"Hey, stranger!" Siena said excitedly.

Does she know it's me? I thought. I was shocked at how happy she sounded that I was calling. "He...Hey, Siena. Do you know who you're speaking with? It's T—"

"Of course I know who this is." She replied with the same excitement in her voice. "It's Taevonne. But you still didn't answer my question, sexy. How are you?" She asked.

I smiled. "I'm doing ok, I guess." I told her honestly. I took a sip of wine and looked toward my bedroom door. "Just wanted to hear the voice of someone nice."

"That doesn't sound good." She said. "How are you...really?" She asked like she truly wanted to know.

I was nervous before I called but there was something about her voice that told me I could talk to her. "Well, actually...I've been better." I was still beating around the bush because it was hard being honest. It was hard being honest with anybody because truthfully this whole situation was embarrassing.

"What does that mean, Tae?" She asked. "I know we just met, but we got pretty acquainted with each other in the little time we've known one another if you catch my meaning, so don't be shy." She giggled. "Talk to me. I want to be a friend to you if I can."

I took a huge sip of wine and a deep breath. "It's just this whole thing with my husband Bronco. I mean, again, I agreed to be open with our sexual relationship together, but I feel like I'm on the outside looking in." I admitted. "I mean like literally, right now we have someone here but all she cares about is him. And it seems like that's all he's focused on too."

"Oh, wow." She paused. "Sometimes in these situations, it takes a little getting use to one another before everyone gels together." She said. "Maybe that's what's going on there."

"But, that wasn't the case when you were here."

"Yeah, but you gotta remember, we got to know each other for a while most of that day. Did you and this other woman get that same opportunity?" She asked.

"No, we just met her at the club tonight. No time for talking or anything just straight to the bed." I explained.

"See, that's why. I'm sure she has no idea that you are new to this and need a little more attention." Siena said.

Wow. She knew exactly how I was feeling and she's not even here. "I think you're right. I really wish it were you with us now and not her." I sighed deeply. "I don't even remember her name." I confessed taking my last sip of wine.

She giggled. "I am here, Tae." She paused. "I'm here with you now on the phone silly." She joked.

"You know what I mean." I said.

"Well, it sounds like you need to get out and talk. And it just so happens that I'm a great listener." I smiled again. "How about you meet me for lunch?" She asked.

I looked at the bedroom door again. I heard Bronco grunting now and the chick screaming. "Sure, is tomorrow good for you?" I asked excitedly.

"Just tell me what time and I promise I'll be there."

CHAPTER ELEVEN

TAE

I cannot believe I agreed to do this. I thought as I pulled on the door that led to the restaurant and movie theatre that Siena and I chose to meet up at in Virginia. I'm not sure why she picked this spot. It was forty-five minutes away from where I lived. And then there was the fact that I was having serious doubts about this outing. The thing was now that I had shown up, maybe I should have just turned around and gone home. I didn't even tell Bronco where I was going.

"Hey, Taevonne." Siena said walking up behind me. I guess it was too late for me to dip out. Damn.

"Hey there," I said awkwardly. She leaned in and gave me a hug. As always she smelled just as good as I remembered and she was as pretty as ever. "Have you been here long?" I asked.

"No, just got here a few minutes before you." She seemed to be looking through me instead of at me and it made me feel wanted. "I got our tickets already." She handed me mine.

"Oh, ok, how much do I owe you?" I asked reaching into my purse to get my money.

She placed her hand on top of mine, stopping me from grabbing my wallet. "Please, it's on me." She smiled.

"Wow." I tried not to blush but it was hard. "Thank you, Siena. That's very sweet of you." I exhaled and she snaked her arm around mine as we walked into the movie.

"It's my pleasure." She looked at the theatre door behind me. "Well, let's go in and get seated. The waiter will come and take our orders in there." She paused. "You're really gonna like this place."

I knew it could be considered wrong for me to be here alone with Siena, but we were just hanging out. Plus I needed someone to talk to who understood my situation and didn't judge it and she was it. Besides, as

By KEESHIA K.

far as I'm concerned it's nothing wrong with that. At least that's what I told myself.

When we got inside we sat in our seats and an usher came over and took our drink order. He also gave us menus to select our meals. "I didn't know they served alcohol here too." I whispered to Siena although there was no one else in the theatre with us.

"Yep, that's why I love this spot. Alcohol and great food brought right to you while you enjoy a movie. Wait until you taste their chicken and waffles. That's what I'm ordering, so you can sample mine if you want." She told me as she stared into my eyes and smiled seductively.

I smiled back and my stomach fluttered. *What have I gotten myself into?* Whatever it was, for now I'm going along for the ride.

AN HOUR LATER

Our food came out, the movie started and we were on our third drink. Her choice was a vodka martini and I stuck with merlot. I couldn't even tell you what the movie was about because I was staring at her. When I wasn't doing that we were talking to each other about everything but what was on the movie screen. We were having so much fun just being in each other's company.

"So, now that you are all liquored up, do you wanna talk about Bronco?" Siena whispered to me.

What's so crazy was ever since I got there and around her, I wasn't even thinking about my husband. It's like all the hurt I felt before going there went away for the time being and I didn't want to ruin it by bringing him up at all.

By KEESHIA K.

I sighed. "No, I'm having too much fun. Besides, I'm not even thinking about him." I shrugged. "But tell the truth, did you rent out this theatre today so we could be alone?" I asked looking around at the dark empty theatre at an attempt to change the subject.

"No, Tae." She paused. "But I will confess that I knew coming to this spot in the early afternoon on a weekday normally meant it could be a ghost town." She stared at me intensely before leaning in and whispering in my ear. "How else would I have you all to myself?" She said, her warm breath tickled. "Plus I thought you needed to talk and wanted you to have the privacy."

I don't know if it was the wine and the atmosphere or the fact that I was mad at Bronco, but I wanted to kiss Siena so bad. I watched her take a sip from her glass and remembered how soft her lips felt on my clit. The memory sent chills up my spine.

Fuck it, Bronco wasn't thinking about me when he spent two hours alone fucking club chick while I was in the living room. So why should I think about him now?

"Would you be offended if I kissed you?" I asked Siena breathing heavily. I was nervous but I really needed to feel loved again. Not only that but I wanted the answer to a question I had been asking myself. Was I gay? Or just gay for my bae?

She didn't say anything after my question. Instead, she put my hair behind my ear and stared into my eyes. The butterflies in my stomach were doing the milly rock. Just when I felt like I would explode she leaned in and pressed her lips against mine. My clit jumped. Why was I so turned on by this woman?

As our tongues danced inside each other's mouths with nothing but the light from the movie screen shining upon our faces, highlighting our indiscretion, she was everything I needed at the moment.

Siena reached down into my tights and moved my thong to the side and played with my soaked clit. Her touch was so soft and sensual, way different from Bronco's and I felt in ecstasy.

When she was done she pulled away from our kiss and whispered in my ear. "I wanna taste you." She seemed to beg as she made her request. Then she did something that almost made me cum in my seat. She pulled her finger out of my pussy and licked it clean.

That did it for me and I was ready to do all I could to have sex with her.

IN THE CAR

We left the theatre and were in the back seat of her truck. The windows were fogged because we both were breathing so heavily. She parked on the far side of the lot and there weren't many cars around us.

Trembling softly, my legs were spread wide and she was sucking my clit sending small waves of pleasure throughout my body. "MMmmmmm....Siena, you feel so good. I needed this so bad. Don't stop." I said running my hands through her long hair.

Just when I felt like I was about to lose control she reached up and grabbed my breasts. I winded softly against her lips, trying not to feel like such a freak but also wanting to cum. When she squeezed my nipple I could no longer hold back and exploded my juices all over her face.

I came so hard it felt like it lasted forever. Looking down at her I said, "Oh my God, you were amazing. You…you felt so right." I placed my hand over my chest to slow my breathing but it didn't seem to stop the heaving.

I felt bad because I didn't know what I could do to bring her to climax, but I knew I couldn't go down on her. I didn't think I was ready for that yet. "What can I…what can I do for you?"

She smiled. "Nothing. I'm going to scissor you." She winked although I had no clue what she meant, but it looked like I was getting ready to find out.

By KEESHIA K.

She turned her body around and slid her legs alongside mine. My head was near her feet and her head was near my feet. We looked like we were in the 69 position sideways but our pussy's were aligned on each other perfectly.

When she began grinding her body, I knew two things. One, she was a pro at this shit and two; I was approaching my second orgasm for the evening.

BACK AT HOME

As I reached my apartment door, the guilt I felt weighed on my back like a ton of bricks. It was later than I normally came home and I knew Bronco was going to wonder where I'd been. I had no idea what I would tell him either. Because if I was honest about seeing Siena, I think he would be angry. But on the other hand if I lie, then I went behind his back.

You know what though, this whole situation was his idea in the first place. I mean I didn't set out to have sex with another woman until he made us. So why should I feel bad? I also knew one thing, while I enjoyed being with Siena, more than I enjoyed anything in a long time, I don't know if I'm gay. What I do know is that with her, I'd be willing to find out.

I continued with the questions in my head as I walked through the door. Whatever mental drama he threw at me, I would just have to deal with. But when I looked around, I noticed the apartment was empty. I glanced down at my watch and I saw that it was 10PM and Bronco wasn't home.

Wow. If only he knew.

116   *By KEESHIA K.*

CHAPTER TWELVE
BRONCO

"I'm telling you, homie, just be straight with these broads and you too can have the dream life." I said to my nosey coworkers. "My wife goes and gets 'em and I fucks 'em, straight like that. To be honest our teamwork makes the dream work."

I was on the job changing the oil on a silver Cadillac Escalade and giving the niggas I work with, Randy and Quentin some hope for they boring ass love lives and future. Part of the reason they didn't have exciting lives was because they were afraid to take chances.

Randy was real tall and lanky and he didn't do nothing to keep himself up. I caught him on the streets one time and he was wearing his uniform even though he was off.

Quentin was a little better I guess. He thought he was the shit because he had that soft hair that females liked and favored the singer, *Miguel,* except he was a couple inches taller. But unless he was getting pussy like me then it didn't mean shit.

"Ain't no way." Randy yelled out laughing like I wasn't trying to give him the gospel. "That may be your thing but it ain't me." He paused. "But to each his own though."

"You say that now but this shit lit," I told him. "I legit wish you could have it like me." I wiped my hands on an oily rag. "We go out to the club and I scope out the spot. I point out the broad I want and wifey goes hunting. Real live." I embellished a little. "The best thing I could've done was marry her."

My co-workers continued to laugh. It was a fairly slow workday. Normally it would be busier than it was so I took advantage of the down time.

"So how did you get her to do that shit?" Quentin walked up to me and asked. "Because I saw her a few times when she came by to scoop you and to be honest she didn't look like the type."

By KEESHIA K.

"Easy, I told her on the day of our wedding that if I couldn't have excitement in the bedroom then we couldn't get married." I paused. "I knew for a fact I wasn't going into the future with lies."

"And she went for that?" Randy asked scratching his head. "Because that seems a little far fetched."

"We married ain't we?" I shot back. "She just lucky I ain't demand we put that shit in our vows." I laughed. "But her family was in the room so that would've been a little awkward."

"So she just gives you a pass to fuck other women?" Q asked looking at me with his arms folded.

"Naw, not on the solo tip." I paused. "We have a threesome with the chicks we bring home." I continued. "And it ain't like it's just me. She be into it too. It's like I awakened something in her that may have always been there."

They both fell out in hysterical laughter I could tell not believing me. That's why I'm glad I had proof.

"I knew niggas would think I was bullshitting...check this out." I snatched off the glove from my hand and reached into my coveralls for my cell phone. After scrolling through my pictures, I found the selfies that I took of me, Siena and Tae. "Look," I said handing Randy my phone. "Now talk that dumb shit." I waited.

He scrolled and Q walked near him to view the snapshots too. I ain't have no nudes or nothing, but the flicks we took do show how close we all were. I figured it would validate me a little at least.

"Oh, shit." Randy yelled. "You serious 'bout this shit?" He continued as he kept scrolling through my phone.

"I told you." I said reaching out for him to hand me my phone back. "I wish I had a pic of the other chick we picked up recently but I ain't get a chance to get none. Besides, she was too worried about the dick for me to take a flick. Maybe I'll catch her next time."

Quentin looked at me with a serious expression. "You need to be careful about this situation, Bronco." He said. "That's all I'm saying."

"Fuck you talking 'bout?" I asked him.

"I'm talking about karma." Quentin shook his head. "Putting your wife in this predicament ain't cool man and if you not careful, it may backfire in your face and she could leave you." He continued. "I've seen this kind of thing happen before."

"First off you lying," I said. "You never seen *this* type of thing before." This nigga sounded like he was hating a little. It's always one in every bunch. "Never!" I reiterated. "If she wasn't down with it she would have never gone through with the wedding. She into it just as much as I am, trust me."

"You ain't leave her no choice by pulling that shit out your ass on your wedding day. That was foul even for you."

"She could've still told me no." I shot back.

He shook his head. "Yeah, aight. But don't say I ain't warn you." He continued turning around to focus on his paperwork.

Randy handed me a quart of oil and I lowered the Escalade to fill it up. Just as I sat the truck back down on the ground, our manager walked past the garage and into the break room.

"I'ma grab a soda. I'll be right back." I told Randy as I jogged towards the break room. She had just paid for pretzels. "You snack on them joints now and you gonna ruin your dinner." I said to my manager, Alicia trying to spark up some convo. She was a little on the sexy side with her caramelized skin and thick pink lips.

"These pretzels are my dinner tonight," she said rolling her eyes. I didn't know why but something told me she wasn't checking for me. "Anyway I have a lot of paperwork to get finished so I'll be working through dinner." She continued focusing back on the machine.

"Oh, yeah, well you know I can stay and give you some assistance if need be." I licked my lips and rubbed my hands together. "You don't have to do it alone." I shrugged.

She laughed. "No, I'm good on that. But what you can do is finish up that Escalade so the customer will be satisfied. I'd like to let him know he can pick it up tonight instead of tomorrow. How 'bout we do that?" She said taking the pretzels out the machine.

I laughed as I watched her walk back into her office. She don't give me no love. I had been trying to get at her ever since she transferred here and became our new manager. But so far nothing I did worked.

She don't wear a wedding ring so I don't think she's married. She ain't even got no Gram or Twitter page. I tried looking her up to see if she got a nigga or something to explain why she so icy. But as of now all my research ended in vain. The only thing I was sure of is that she didn't fuck with me.

I grabbed a soda and walked back out into the garage where I saw Randy laughing. He must have seen me fail at trying my hand but I didn't give a fuck. Quentin looked over at me and shook his head. Fuck that nigga! All I knew was this, I had to get at her. *At the end of the day I won't give up until she caves. Believe that.*

I opened my soda and started hatching up a plan.

By KEESHIA K.

CHAPTER THIRTEEN

TAE

I was eating dinner at home in the living room while on the phone with Siena. Although we texted each other every day, this was the first time I had spoken to her since our sex/lunch at the movies.

"So, what happened?" I asked nosily. Siena was telling me the story of what went on in her last relationship. "Because I don't get why you're single. Something ain't adding up."

She giggled. "Let's just say that my ex was crazy. She did stupid things all the time and we would go back and fourth in the relationship. But the final straw was when I had to get stitches after a fight. I knew I wasn't going to be with a person who hit me." She explained.

"Wait a minute…what?" I asked putting my fork down. "You had to get stitches because she hit you? I didn't even know lesbians went through that kind of stuff too."

"Yep, she had hit me before, but this time the stitches were because she bit me on my back." She continued. "The bite was so deep that it looked crazy even after it was sewn up. I had to have reconstructive surgery to fix it and everything." She informed.

"Oh my God! How on earth did she bite you that hard on your back to cause that much damage?" I asked puzzled.

"Like I said we had an argument, and it was bad. It lasted for a couple days and we didn't speak to each other at all." She paused. "So we eventually came back together to talk it out as we did often when we had a fight." She paused. "But this time, after we yelled it out, we got turned on. Which is something we also did a lot of, fighting and fucking."

I listened attentively. She didn't strike me as the type of woman to put up with this kind of drama so I was curious how it all played out.

126   *By KEESHIA K.*

"Anyway, while we were in the middle of a heavy sex session, she just hauled off and bit a chunk out my back. Here I was thinking we were making up and she was still mad the entire time." She sighed. "The way she did it was so devious though."

"That is so crazy." I told her. "I'm so sorry. I can't believe you went through something like that." I paused. "How long were you guys together before you officially broke it off?"

"Off and on for a year." She said.

"Well where is she now? I mean, do you still see her?" I asked chewing my chicken slowly so I didn't make smacking noises over the phone. "Because I would try to avoid her if I was you."

"Uh...No. She actually died." She said in a low voice.

I started choking on my dinner. I did not expect her to tell me that. "What...How?" I asked while coughing.

"I don't know all the details." She paused. "She was on her way home and someone stabbed her I think." She said in a low voice. "It's a mystery to this day for real."

I took a sip of water and cleared my throat. "Wow, I really am so sorry, Siena." I said. "I know you guys were broken up, but I can't imagine how you felt when you found out." I continued. "Because at some point I know you cared about her."

I heard keys jingling at the front door and looked at it. Seconds later Bronco walked in from work and shook his head when he saw me sitting on the couch on the phone. He didn't say anything to me, just walked towards the kitchen with an attitude all over his face.

"How long ago did this happen?" I asked Siena not caring about Bronco's screwed up face. To be honest I was kind of tired of kissing up to him. Sometimes he acted like a kid and needed to grow up.

"Over a year ago." Siena said. "It was real hard for me the first few months after she passed but I got over

128   *By KEESHIA K.*

it." She continued. "I think her family took it hard though. Her mother had a heart attack. Her father had a stroke. It was real bad."

"What the fuck is this?" Bronco walked up behind me and asked. When I turned around he was holding the Fried Chicken salad I made us for dinner in his hand.

"Wow…Um can you hold on for a sec?" I asked Siena but didn't wait to hear her reply before I pushed the mute button on my cell phone. "It's dinner, Bronco what you think it is?" I asked him.

"This it?" He frowned. "Because I need more than this." He said with an attitude holding the plate up. "I mean you normally make me some wings or some burgers or something to go along with the salad, Tae. This not gonna hold me up all night."

"I made cornbread too, it's in the oven." I paused. "But I didn't make anything else because I'm trying to cut back on the stuff we eat around here. Plus that salad has a lot of substance in it and its healthier for us." I told him turning back around to finish my conversation.

"Man, fuck all that." He said waving me off. "I worked all day long and I expect to come home to more to eat than this bird food you trying to give me." He yelled. "You know I do manual labor."

I ignored him and focused on the phone. I hit the mute button again so that I could talk. "My bad. Anyway, I know that was rough to go through. I can't even imagine." I said to Siena not checking for Bronco anymore. I knew he was being extra because I was still on the phone even though he was home.

"It was a crazy time believe me," she sighed. "Anyway, I know Bronco home now and I don't wanna keep you." Siena paused. "So just text me when you can and I'll talk to you later."

I sighed not really wanting to deal with him and his temper tantrum at the moment. "I guess...ok, that's cool. Talk to you soon." I ended the call and put my cell phone face down on the couch before picking up the remote to turn the TV on.

I felt Bronco staring at me from behind. The tension was so thick, I thought the steam coming out of him would burn the back of my neck but I refused to turn around and look at him.

I don't know what came over me all of a sudden. But I felt different in ways I couldn't explain. Maybe I was still holding on to anger from the night I came home late and he wasn't even there. Or maybe it was everything that's been going on with us since we got married. I couldn't put my finger on it, but I just didn't feel like it with him tonight.

"Who the fuck was that on the phone?" He finally asked. "Had to be somebody real important for you not to get off the call once I came in. I mean we are married."

I turned around and laughed loudly. It took me a few seconds to calm down and he was glaring the entire time. "Bronco, I don't ask you who you be on the phone with do I?"

"That's cuz I don't be on that bitch!" He yelled. "You must be out here fucking around or something. If you are say it. Because it's obvious that you want to."

"You playing right?" I asked getting up to walk towards him. I couldn't believe he was asking me something like that.

"No I ain't playing." He continued.

I just looked at him. He had some nerve with all the shit I been putting up with around here. "You know what, fuck all this shit. It don't even matter to me." Feeling like I didn't owe him an explanation, I walked past him and headed to our bedroom giggling the entire way.

IN THE KITCHEN
BRONCO

By KEESHIA K.

What the fuck just happened here? Did Tae really just carry the shit out of me and not answer none of my questions? I thought. Something is definitely going on with her and this new attitude. For her sake, she better hope I never find out she cheating on me.

I'll light this entire bitch up.

CHAPTER FOURTEEN

BRONCO

I made Tae bring me to work today for a couple reasons but mainly so that I could introduce her to my manager. I wanted to see if she could help me get ole girl in the sack. For some reason I needed to bust them cheeks bad. And the urge wouldn't go away.

When Tae pulled up I pointed to the parking space in the lot so that she could park the truck, which was not too far from the entrance. She looked at me like I was crazy but I just pointed harder. Sometimes she acts like an idiot so I have to treat her like one.

I had been outside my building smoking my Capone while I waited on her to come scoop me. After she parked she sat there and played with her phone. Every few seconds she would look up at me and smile but I felt like something was different. Especially after how she treated me the night before. In the past, whenever I came home she was always available for me but last night she acted funny so something was definitely up.

I walked toward my ride to get Tae. I came up on the driver's side and tapped the window with my knuckles so she could roll it down. "Why you ain't get out?" I asked. "You acting all anti-social and shit."

"Get out for what, Bronco?" She frowned. "I've never gotten out when I picked you up from work before. Why should that change now?" She paused. "I mean are you not ready to go?"

I laughed. She was right, normally there was no reason for her to do anything but pull up, but today, I had bigger plans. Plans I needed her help with if I was going to fulfill my goal.

"I know." I said using my knuckle to touch her cheek. "I just wanted to introduce you to my new manager." I paused and flicked the end of my Capone and blew out the last of the smoke. "So get out."

She frowned. "Introduce me...for what?" She paused looking puzzled. "Because I'm not in the mood."

"You not in the mood?" I repeated with an attitude. "I want you to get out cuz, I wanted you to get acquainted with her if you catch my drift." I told her smiling. "Stop playing stupid. You know what it is."

Her jaw hung. "Are you serious, Bronco?" She paused. "You really want me to play this game with you on your job?" She asked like I ain't know where the fuck we were.

"Yeah, I'm serious. I know where I am. And like I said I still want you to come on to her." I paused. "You ain't gotta be aggressive like you were with the club chicks but just hint around and feel her out." I coached. "See if she's the type to be interested because I have a good feeling about her."

She dropped her head down and took a deep breath. "I'm not even dressed for all this, Bronco. I mean I been at work all day." She told me. "I really

By KEESHIA K.

thought I was picking you up and going back home to prepare dinner."

"You look fine, Tae. It ain't like you proposing to shawty, just a little harmless flirting is all." I said opening the truck door so she could get out. "Now let's go. You wasting time."

She took off her seat belt and checked her hair and face in the sun visor mirror. "You are really something else, you know that?" She said stepping out of the truck. She had on a pair of jeans that I loved how her ass looked in. If that ass don't get at shawty nothing will.

MANAGER'S OFFICE

TAE

I was really becoming annoyed with what Bronco kept asking me to do. I mean now he has me trolling for sex at his job...When will this end? It's like he was doing all he could to break me and I wondered to myself how much more of this I could take.

KNOCK. KNOCK. KNOCK.

We were outside of an office and I was so frustrated my breath was heavy. It was like I was running a race. "Come in," a female's voice from inside yelled out. Bronco opened the door and we walked into his manager's office.

"Alicia, I know you busy. But I wanted you to meet my wife, Taevonne. Tae, this is my manager, Alicia." Bronco said. I was getting nervous and felt like I was on the verge of one of my panic attacks again. This was all so ridiculous. There seemed to be no ending to what he was capable of.

Trying to prevent further embarrassment, I took a deep breath and walked up to her. "Hello, it's very nice to meet you." I reached out to shake her hand. "I was just picking up Bronco and decided to stop in and say hello. I hope that's okay."

"Of course it's fine, Taevonne." She said smiling and grabbing my hand. There was a brief second of silent awkwardness. "I was just going over some paperwork. Nothing too heavy."

"Uh, Alicia, Tae was telling me that she wanted to get her hair done in them temporary locs and I told her that your hair was like that. So I figured I would hook ya'll up with each other so she can get hers done too." Bronco said lying. "Especially since yours looks so nice."

"Oh, ok." She touched her hair. "Well, actually I did them myself." Alicia said looking at me. "It takes a while to do, but it's worth it in the end. As long as you can maintain them."

"Yeah, Tae, you stay here and chat with Alicia and I'll go grab my bag and meet you at the truck." Bronco said smiling. "Ain't no need in me being in no female conversation, feel me?"

I turned around and looked at him and he winked and smiled bigger. I rolled my eyes and turned back around to face Alicia. I can't believe he is actually doing this. I feel like I'm in a bad dream.

There was more awkward silence as I searched my brain trying to find the right words to say without coming on too strong. The last thing I wanted was for her to get offended and take it out on Bronco. He needed this job. We needed his job which is why this was a dumb ass move.

"Uhhh, ummm do you do other people's heads or just your own?" I managed to ask her. My palms were beginning to sweat.

"I have done a head or two." She leaned back in her chair like I was asking for a job, but not really in a nasty way. As if she were trying to figure me out or something. "I don't make it my business, but sometimes I don't mind." She continued.

"Oh...Um, so would you mind coming to my place and doing my hair?" I said with a half smirk trying my best to lightly flirt and not throw up all over her paperwork. "I mean, if you have the time."

By KEESHIA K.

She didn't answer.

She just smiled at me and walked over to her office door and closed it softly. I cut my eyes towards the window where the blinds were open and I could see Bronco staring at us from the door leading to the parking lot.

"Listen, Taevonne, can I call you Tae?" She asked softly. I nodded my head yes. Too weirded out to say much more. "I know what's going on here but what I don't understand is why?"

"Excuse me?" I asked in a low voice. "I'm not sure what you mean. I wanted to get my hair done and—"

"So Bronco told you to come in here and flirt with me...Am I right?" She asked. "You're here now so you might as well be honest. Besides, anything other than the truth is a waste of time for both of us."

My eyes bugged out in shock. How did she know? "Ummm, how—"

"I overheard him bragging to some of the mechanics about how you guys bring women home." She explained. I was so humiliated. I looked away and dropped my head in shame. "I'ma be straight with you because I think you need to hear it and I got time today." She started. "I don't know you, shit, I barely know him, but I know his kind and I can see that he's a jerk. And as pretty as you are and kind as you appear to be, it just seems like a wrong fit."

She walked closer to where I stood. "You need to get rid of him, Tae. You're too beautiful to be fetching pussy for a man. If he wants to do those things then let him have at it and leave you out of it."

I took a deep breath and tried to fight the tears I felt forming back. "You don't understand. If I…If I don't do what he asks he'll leave me." I finally looked up at her. "And I can't have that."

She shook her head slowly. "I can see this will get worse before it gets better but I also know you won't make any changes until you're ready." She took a deep breath. "So, since I know he's an ass and I know he's watching I'll do you a favor." She moved even closer to

By KEESHIA K.

me. She lifted my chin and stared into my eyes and whispered into my ear. Then she leaned in and kissed me on the cheek. "Leave him before he destroys you so much you won't be able to."

IN THE TRUCK

TAE

"Damn, bae, ya'll looked so good in there with each other." He smiled slyly, rubbing his hands together. "I knew that shit would work." Bronco laughed into his fist. "So when she coming through?" He asked. "Tonight, tomorrow? When? If she coming tonight we have to go to the store and—"

"She's not coming, Bronco." I said bursting his bubble. "She told me that she thinks I'm sexy but...that she's not attracted to you at all. I can't be sure but I actually think she believes you're gross."

Bronco's nose flared and his temples popped out like they always did when he was angry.

I knew he was mad and probably even embarrassed, but if I was being honest it felt good to get turned down this time. Especially by her. I knew that he was humiliated that he took his shot and missed. Maybe now he would finally feel how I do all the time when he sends me on these pussy quests.

Having annihilated his feelings for a change, I smiled slightly to myself and pulled out of the parking lot and drove home.

By KEESHIA K.

CHAPTER FIFTEEN

TAE

I can't really tell if Bronco is still mad about his manager kissing me and dismissing him or not. I mean he hasn't had too much convo for me around the house, but that's no big surprise. Lately, he hadn't really said a lot anyway. And for some reason I didn't care.

I'll know for sure if he's still mad when we go out tonight. A couple days before that fiasco at his job he told me we were going to the lounge. So if he's good and not tripping off his manager then we'll go. If not he'll make an excuse. I guess I'll have to wait and see.

I was sitting in the living room on the couch while I flipped through Netflix movies when Bronco walked into the apartment. He had been out playing ball with some friends.

"Tae, why you ain't getting dressed?" He asked putting his basketball in the hall closet. He was sweaty but looked good enough to eat if I was in the mood. And I think I was. Sometimes I got turned on when he walked through the door after a game. "You know we going out."

I guess everything was cool. "Oh, I forgot." I told him lying. "I'll get dressed but come here for a second."

"Naw, bae, I gotta jump in the shower. You know a nigga been running and shit all day." He said trying to walk past me and toward the bathroom.

I jumped up off the couch and stood in his way. I wanted to taste him. It was something about him glistening with sweat after his basketball games that got my pussy tingling. "I said come here, Bronco." I gripped his dick and tugged it slightly. When I had a hold of him I pushed him down on the couch and stood over him.

"Damn, Tae," he said already stiffening within my hand. I snatched his shorts and boxer briefs down and stroked him into full stiffness before I stuffed him in

146   *By KEESHIA K.*

my mouth. He threw his head back and grabbed my hair.

I don't know what came over me. Maybe I was checking his temperature to see if we were really cool. Or maybe I was trying to see if I was still attracted to him or not. Whatever it was took over me completely and had me playing the role of slutty housewife.

I sucked him off so good that within minutes he gripped my head and let out a loud growl. Then he shot his load into my throat. I slurped up all his juices and wiped my mouth with the back of my hand. "Now, I'll get dressed." I said standing up smiling and walking to the bathroom.

THE LOUNGE
TAE

We were sitting in the VIP section of the lounge and were already on our third drinks. Not only did I look good, but I felt even better. I was out with my husband and truly enjoying his company and it gave me hope that maybe things would be okay. These were the moments I cherished the most.

"Hey, you tipsy over there ain't you." Bronco asked me smiling. I adored his smile. He is so fucking sexy when he's happy.

"I must admit, I do feel good." I said laughing and tapping my foot to *Drip* by Cardi B and Migos. "Its like this entire night has been perfect." I paused. "Thank you, Bronco."

"Good…good, I'm glad you feeling it. Now go over to the bar and bring shawty back to me." Bronco said looking in the direction of a woman at the bar. When I followed his eyes I saw a cute chick with big titties staring back at him. "Work ain't gonna be hard, she been looking this way since we got here." He continued. "This one should be smooth sailing."

By KEESHIA K.

My jaw hung and I looked the woman over. She was short and thick with braids. She wasn't Bronco's typical type but she did have a nice shape. I took a deep breath. It seemed like just when I thought shit was cool, he cashed in his get *some free pussy card*...again. I got up, smoothed out my skirt and walked over to her. Besides, there was no use in arguing.

"Hey, you want to come join my husband and me at our table?" I asked secretly hoping she said no.

"Sure." She said excitedly. "I was sitting over here bored anyway. Thanks for the invitation." She was just a little bit too happy to get over there to Bronco if you asked me but whatever.

I grabbed her hand and we walked across the floor to our table where Bronco was eagerly waiting. "So what's your name?" I asked.

"V," she said never looking away from Bronco.

"Bronco, this is V." I paused. "V, this is my husband Bronco." I introduced them. Bronco moved over on the couch and motioned for V to sit next to him by patting the empty space several times.

I walked around to the other side of him and attempted to sit down until he stopped me. "Look, uh, Tae I'm going to get to know V here for a little bit on my own." He winked. "Why don't you go and do a spin around the dance floor or something. Ain't nothing wrong with exercise, plus you been sitting down all night." He said turning around to look at V.

I laughed. "Bronco stop playing." I reached for the Vodka and tried to sit down again. "Move over."

"I'm not fucking playing." He said snapping his neck back around to face me. His voice was stern and serious. "Go. Don't make me say it again." He paused and looked at me. "You still here?"

I looked at him like he had two heads. I looked over at V but she cut her eyes away from me fast like she was embarrassed for me.

"Whatever, Bronco." I turned and walked away from the table. I have never been more humiliated in

By KEESHIA K.

my life. I guess I got my answer though. He was still angry about Alicia turning him down and he was taking it out on me.

2 HOURS LATER
BRONCO

This V chick breath stinks! I tried my hardest to ignore it, but it's too powerful. I even gave her ass a Life Saver thinking it would help, but nah. If I was taking score it would be her breath one, Life Saver zero.

Breath or not, her titties were huge and they gave me something to look at. Before this night was over, I looked forward to putting my dick in between 'em for sho. And as whorish as she was acting it would be easy.

After I got her ready to go, it was time to go find my wife and bring her back over to the VIP. I gather after two hours of banishment she's learned her lesson by now. I know I was wrong for kicking her out the way I did, but she embarrassed me in front of my manager. She knew she was wrong too, that's why she threw me that charity head earlier. She must think I'm stupid.

"Look, I'll be right back," I said to V. "Don't go nowhere." I winked at her and got up and walked across the dance floor. Rubbing my hands together I scanned the place. "Where are you, Tae?"

The DJ was in a throwback vibe and was playing back to back *Jodeci*. Tae loved that group so I knew she was somewhere in here dancing and probably singing at the top of her lungs. I chuckled.

I looked all around the floor and didn't see Tae. I was just about to go on the other side of the lounge to check for her when I spotted a familiar face across the room.

By KEESHIA K.

It was me and Tae's first quest. *Damn, Siena looking good.* My mind traveled back to the fun her, Tae and me had not too long ago and I was getting turned on. Shit, if I had my choice we going home with that tonight. Fuck Breathy McBig Titty.

I picked up my pace to catch up with Siena. She had two drinks in her hand so I was trying to cut her off before she got back to whichever nigga she was in here with.

But I stopped dead in my tracks when she made it back to a VIP section and I saw who was sitting on the couch grabbing the other drink out her hand. It was Tae.

I stood there and watched them for a minute puzzled. They laughed and looked at each other like no one else was in the room. They seemed extra comfortable around one another as if no time had passed since our sexcapade. Curious, I headed over to see what was up.

"Damn, Tae, why you ain't come and tell me you ran into our friend." I smiled observing ole girl while rubbing my hands together. "Aye, what's good, Siena? How you been?" I licked my lips.

"Hey, Bronco." She waved and cleared her throat, before looking at Tae. "How you doing?" Siena took a sip out her drink.

"I'm good, now that you here." I said throwing it on strong. Thinking back to how tight and wet her pussy was had me ready to leave right now. "I don't know what you getting into tonight but—"

"Siena, let's go." Tae said cutting me off and standing up. She reached down and grabbed her purse. "The air got stank all of a sudden."

"You must be reading my mind." I said rubbing my hands together. "I'll go bring the truck around and—"

Tae laughed hard. "Don't bother, Bronco." She told me as she grabbed Siena's hand and tried to walk past me.

Heated, I snatched her arm roughly, spinning her back around to face me. "What the fuck you doing?" It took everything in me to hold back from smacking the shit out of her in this club. "Why you disrespecting like this?"

She yanked her arm out of my grasp. "Fuck you, Bronco. Go get to know V a little more, ain't that what you wanted to do?"

Tae turned around and walked away. Siena smiled as she pulled her toward the exit leaving me standing there with my mouth open.

"The fuck?"

CHAPTER SIXTEEN
BRONCO

I was back at my spot with V, angry fucking her from the back. Shit, I wasn't about to waste the connection Tae made when she hooked us up, even if she did. Besides, V was primed and ready to go at the club. Except instead of it being her, Tae and me, it was just her and me.

Some shit ain't sit right with this whole Siena situation. I mean, they looked awfully close and familiar with each other. I was starting to think her being at the lounge tonight wasn't a coincidence.

"Open that ass up, V," I said as I smacked her butt cheek. Shawty was mediocre at best in bed because she had no idea how to take dick. I feel like I'm coaching and I ain't plan on all that tonight.

"Like this, baby?" V asked me while grabbing both sides of her ass cheeks and pulling them apart roughly.

By KEESHIA K.

Nah, not like that. I thought to myself. I rolled my eyes and continued to plow into her. I was pumping so hard that her pussy started making the fart noise. Too much air had gotten in there and she was dry. If only she knew how to work her pussy we wouldn't have this problem. This fuck would be so much more enjoyable. Instead, all I'm thinking about is Tae.

Fuck this, I'm ready to bust this nut and hitting shawty off like this ain't gonna do it for me. I pulled my dick out and snatched off the condom. "Turn over." I told her.

She rolled over off her knees and onto her back. I climbed on top of her and straddled her stomach and chest. I placed my dick in between her huge titties.

She looked up at me puzzled like I stuck it in her ear or something. "What's wrong? You ain't never been titty fucked before?" I asked looking down at her.

She shook her head no. Damn this bitch was blowing me. I might as well have come home by myself and jerked off. "It's easy, just squeeze your titties around my dick and move 'em up and down." I explained.

She started out slow but steady. "Is this good?" She asked looking up at my face for validation. If I could give her anything it was that she was a willing participant.

"Yeah, yeah," I said hoping she'd shut the fuck up. Her breath still stank and it was smacking me in my nose. "Faster." I told her feeling the tingling sensation up my spine that I always felt when my nut was approaching.

She started moving her hands at a quick pace and I knew it wouldn't be long before I shot my load. I pumped into her to help speed up the process and after a good 5 strokes I bust my nut all on her chin. Shit, she wouldn't be half bad at this if she had a little more practice. Just not with me.

Tired, I rolled off her and layed down on the bed out of breath. She turned to face me and pulled me into a strong embrace. Then out of nowhere she started grinding her pussy against my semi soft dick. I was in shock. *What the fuck kinda freaky shit was this?* I thought.

Just when I was about to ask her what the fuck was she doing, she let out a scream so loud I was afraid my neighbors might call the police. I put my hand over her mouth to muffle her yelp just as her body started to convulse. Did this bitch just cum?

"Oh...Oh...My...God, Bronco. I never came that hard before." She said out of breath.

I didn't say anything but that was the weirdest shit I had ever been used sexually for. I quickly pulled out of her crazy grip and rolled onto my other side so that my back was toward her. I grabbed at the sheet and wiped her juices off me.

She threw her leg over mine and snuggled up to my back. "That was fun." She said. "I'm so glad I went to that club tonight."

I wasn't in the mood for small talk so I snatched the sheet up over my shoulder and faked sleep.

30 MINUTES LATER

BRONCO

I heard light snoring coming from behind me so I gently turned over to make sure V was really sleep. When I moved, she shifted slightly too but was still knocked out. I climbed out of bed and looked for my cell phone. I couldn't find it anywhere but then I remembered it was probably in my jeans pocket.

I located my black Levis on the floor and felt around them in search of my phone. We came in here and went right to work buzzed off the liquor. So we took our clothes off so fast that I didn't have time to put my phone on my bed table like I normally did.

When I found it inside my pocket I slowly crept out of the bedroom and into the living room to look for Tae. The apartment was dark and there was no sign

By KEESHIA K.

that she had come home. I unlocked my phone and checked to see if I had any texts or missed calls...I didn't. Wow, it was 3:00 in the morning and not only was Tae not home but she hadn't called or texted me. What kind of shit is this? She never did stuff like this.

Angry, I called her ready to kirk out. The phone rang four times before her voicemail came on. Oh she really carried it now. I was heated. Yeah, I know I treated her like shit at the club but like I said, she had that coming. Still, she not supposed to be going like this.

I threw my phone down on the dining room table and headed back to my bedroom. I looked down at V sleeping and felt my blood boiling. I jumped up on the bed and smooched the shit out the back of her head.

"Hey...what's going on?" V woke up and said. She looked shocked like I punched her in the face or something. "Why you do that?"

"You gotta hit it." I told her as I gathered her clothes off the floor. I wanted this chick the fuck out my crib now. "I'm not feeling like company no more. We did our thing but it's done."

"Wait, what is your problem?" She asked climbing out my bed. She bent down to pick up her shoes. "Did I do something wrong? I thought we had fun and—"

"Ain't no problem but this ain't no bed and breakfast so you gotta dip." I said tossing her dress at her. "Now leave. It's already late."

"Have you lost your fucking mind?" She yelled. "It's the middle of the night and I'm not driving home this late." She pouted.

"So don't go home then, bitch. I truly don't give a fuck where you wander but you leaving up outta here." I shouted.

"I cannot believe this shit." She shook her head. "I can see why your wife ain't come home, dirty nigga. You clearly don't know how to treat a woman." She slid on her dress. "I'm surprised a woman as pretty as her would even marry your busted ass." She shot back.

"You don't know me, whore! Your pussy was trash." I yelled. "Now get your shitty mouth ass the fuck out my crib, bitch! You lucky I ain't put your ass out naked." I walked out the bedroom and into the living room.

She followed me down the hall, zipped up her dress and grabbed her purse. She was huffing and puffing so hard I thought she was about to try and blow my house down. "I thought you were a gentleman but clearly you're an asshole." She yelled.

"Let me show you just how much of a gentleman I can be." I said. I walked over to the front door and held it open for her. "Bounce."

She stomped past me and walked through the door. She had just barely crossed the threshold when I slammed it shut.

"Fuck you!" She yelled from the hallway.

"Whore!" I yelled as I walked back to my empty bedroom.

CHAPTER SEVENTEEN
TAE

"I can't believe he treated me like that...I'm his wife." I cried. I was sobbing my eyes out in Siena's lap. We were at her house lying in her bed and I know it was wrong to be ruining the evening talking about my husband but I couldn't help it. When Bronco decided to carry the fuck out of me at the lounge I called Siena who came to my rescue before we walked out on him and we ended up at her place.

"I'm so sorry, Tae," Siena said rubbing my back. "I wish you weren't going through this pain right now."

I wiped my nose with the balled up tissue I had clutched in my hand. "What makes this worse is I'm not sure who's at fault." I told her sniffing. "Is it him for treating me like that or me for allowing it?"

Siena didn't say anything. She reached over and grabbed more tissue off the bedside table and handed

By KEESHIA K.

it to me. "Don't do this to yourself. It's not worth it and won't help anything."

"No, I'm serious." I said lifting my head off her lap and sitting up next to her. "I really want to know who's at fault, me or him?" I paused. "You can be honest with me."

Siena didn't say anything right away. She cut her eyes away from me and took a sip of water from her glass that was on the nightstand.

"Siena!" I yelled letting her know I really wanted an answer. "Are you gonna be honest with me or not?"

"Listen, it's not my way to put my two cent in when it comes to people's relationships, much less their marriage." She started. "But since you are asking me for my opinion and you aren't taking no for an answer, I'll give it to you." She put her glass back down. "It's both your faults."

"Huh…How is that an answer?" I asked not falling for the cop out she was trying to use.

"He should have never been treating you the way he has." She took a deep breath. "Although if he hadn't I wouldn't have met you." She touched my leg. "At the same time he's been moving like you some side bitch down for whatever and not his wife."

"Exactl—"

"Wait, let me finish." She continued cutting me off. I sat back and leaned against her black leather headboard. "But...he could never have been trying you like he did if you didn't allow it."

I put my head back and stared up at her ceiling while tears streamed down the sides of my face. She placed her hand on my thigh and I looked over at her. "You accepted this lifestyle when you agreed to it at your wedding. To him that was an open invitation to do whatever he wanted with you or, if I'm being very honest, without you too." Siena said. She wiped the tears off my cheeks. "I know it hurts to hear but you asked for honesty."

I dropped my head into my hands and cried harder. She was right...My best friend Stacy was right

By KEESHIA K.

and everyone else who knew about Bronco and my situation were right. I should have never allowed him to bring women into our marriage.

Bronco was taking complete advantage of me because he knew he could. I was never interested in getting women for him to bring back home and fuck with me. The problem now was how do I stop it? I looked over at her. "What am I supposed to do now?" I looked up at Siena and asked. "I mean, I accepted it and now to say no could mean the end."

"And what's wrong with that?" She shrugged. "If you ask me I think you should leave him." She looked at me intensely. "You shouldn't have to put up with his shit, you're too smart and too pretty for that."

Now she sounded just like his boss Alicia. "Leave him and go where? We live together." I said.

"Stay here with me." She replied. "It's not like I don't have the space and I would love to have you."

"Are you serious?" My eyes widened. "I mean, but you barely know me." I was shocked that she even offered.

"We've gotten to know a lot about each other since we met." She laughed. "And when I'm with you I feel like I've known you forever. Plus, you need this, Tae. Or at least some time away from Bronco if nothing else to get a clear mind about what your future holds." She explained. "The invitation is open and I truly don't mind."

I took a deep breath and looked at her. Sitting next to me was a woman who came into my life as a direct result of my husband's demands for our open marriage and yet she was looking out for me more than he ever had.

I nodded my head. "Ok, I'll think about it." I told her honestly. I placed my hand on top of hers. "Thank you for the offer." I smiled. "You don't know how much it means to me."

She pulled me into a deep kiss.

By KEESHIA K.

LATER THAT DAY

TAE

Siena and I were in her kitchen eating. We had been having sex all day long since I told her I would think about staying with her and we were famished. Luckily she ordered pizza and salads and we were devouring them. Having multiple orgasms really worked up an appetite. Who knew?

"I can't believe it's almost 3:00 in the afternoon." I giggled shaking my head. "Where did the time go?" I took a bite of my slice.

"Time really did get away from us." Siena said. "You know it could be like this all the time." She winked. "That is if you want it to be."

I smiled nervously. *What does that mean?* I thought chewing my food slowly as I tried not to make eye contact.

I heard a faint ringing sound coming from the living room. "You hear that?" I asked Siena. I placed my slice down on the plate in front of me.

"Hear what?" She asked. I squinted my eyes and listened harder. It sounded like my cell phone ringing. I jumped up from the table to grab it out of my purse on the couch.

"Oh my, God, it's Bronco." I said as I retrieved my phone and saw his picture flash across the screen.

"So." Siena said dryly. If I'm not mistaken I swore I saw her roll her eyes. "Why should the world stop for him when it didn't stop for you at the club?" She shrugged. "If I were you I wouldn't answer."

I held the phone in my hand and stared down at it. "But I think I should answer it though." I said ready to swipe my finger across the bottom of the screen to accept the call.

By KEESHIA K.

"Wait! You want to answer it? For fucking what?" Siena yelled at me from the kitchen table. "I mean can you really be that stupid?"

Wow. Is she serious? I thought. "I should answer because...well, he *is* my husband and I've been gone all night and most of the day." I told her. I was just about to say hello when out of nowhere a plate came crashing at the wall behind my head.

I jumped from the sound of the glass shattering and looked at Siena while my jaw hung open. She didn't look at me. She just got up from the table, stormed into her bedroom and slammed the door.

What the hell just happened here? I thought feeling super awkward.

CHAPTER EIGHTEEN
BRONCO

I still couldn't believe Tae didn't come home. It ain't like her to carry shit like this. Don't get me wrong. We had our fights but they ain't never been this bad where she would disrespect me. After all, I'm her husband.

I was on my way to work and I can't lie, I had a rough weekend with her being gone. I never realized how much she did for me. I had to wash my own coveralls and fix my meals. Shit I never realized how hard it was to do stuff for myself.

Add to that the fact that I don't even know the first place to look for her. I know she must be with that bitch Siena. But is she gone forever? If she would at least call me I could try and work this shit out somehow, maybe before it was too late.

As I drove down the street in silence my cell phone rung. "Tae," I said out loud thinking it was my wife. I

172 *By KEESHIA K.*

dug my phone out of my pants pocket but saw it was my moms instead.

Fuck!

"What she want this early in the morning?" I asked myself. "Hello." I said, hoping it wasn't bad news.

"Hey, baby...You...you on your way to work?" She asked. Something sounded like it was wrong. "I hate to be bothering you."

"Hey, ma, yeah, I'm headed there now but you good?" I asked hearing the distress in her voice. She didn't sound like herself.

"Yes, uh, that's good. Listen, baby, I'm very proud of you, Bronco. You have really grown into a strong and good man. And I pray that you stay that way too." She said ignoring my question and sounding like she was on the verge of crying.

"Ma...what's up? You never call me this early and you don't sound all that good. Do you need something?" I asked her concerned. "Whatever it is I can call off and help you out."

"No, son. I don't need anything. Like I said you were on my mind and I wanted you to know it. I also wanted to say that I love you very much, baby. Never doubt that, ok?" She asked.

"Aight, ma."

"I gotta go, I'll see you soon." She said and blew a kiss before she ended the call. Something was definitely off. I looked at my phone screen at the time. I didn't have that long before I had to be at work, but by the sound of my mother's voice I needed to go check on her.

So instead of going in I bucked a U in the middle of the block and headed to her house.

By KEESHIA K.

It was creepily quiet as I walked up to my parent's front door. I didn't see my dad's car in the driveway, so I figured he must have already left out for work. That was fine because I didn't feel like seeing his face anyway.

I rung the doorbell first to make sure I didn't surprise her when I came in. But when she didn't answer I grabbed the spare key from under the mat and went inside.

"Ma," I called out to her as I walked through the dining room. I checked the mail to see if anything came for me. I still received mail there from time to time.

"Ma, where are you?" I yelled walking into the kitchen where my mother usually had breakfast cooked. There was nothing on the stove, which shocked me.

I jogged up the steps with an uneasy feeling in my gut. When I got to my mother's room I almost fell back down the stairs. I was right. There my mother was, in the bathtub with her wrists slashed. I ran into the bathroom and tried to stop the bleeding by squeezing her arms.

"Ma, why, why would you do this?!" I yelled. "Help! Help! Somebody fucking help me!" The more I squeezed the more blood oozed out and it was obvious that it was too late.

She was gone.

The coroner just left with my mother's body. I was still sitting in the bathroom on the floor where my mom's blood still dripped down the side of the tub.

She left a note. It was the hardest thing in the world to read but I needed to know why. In the letter she said that she couldn't take the verbal and emotional abuse from my father anymore, but that she loves me very

176   *By KEESHIA K.*

much. She said I was the only bright spot in her life and she would miss me.

All my life I looked away when my pops said or did shit to make my moms feel small. Now, I wished I hadn't. If I had done more and even stuck up for her maybe she would still be alive.

Hurt, I pulled myself up off the floor. But before leaving out the bathroom, I looked over at the tub that no longer held my mother's corpse.

I began to feel a burning sensation take over my whole body. I was heated thinking about how fucked up my pops had been to my moms and it had me wanting to kill that nigga.

Enraged, I ran out the bathroom and bolted down the stairs. When I saw my pops sitting on the arm of the couch crying I rushed his ass knocking him to the floor.

"Fuck you down there crying for, nigga?" I yelled. "You the reason she dead!" I stood over top of him. In my mind I was begging for a reason to beat his ass.

"I'm sorry." He cried. "I never meant, I never meant to hurt her." He continued. He didn't even fight me back. He just lie there balling his eyes out. "Please, please forgive me."

"Don't be sorry now, nigga! You killed her. You treated her like shit. She couldn't take it no more and it's all your fault! I wish your ass would have died instead of her." I was beside myself with anger. I wanted to kill him. I wanted him to feel all the hurt and pain that he made my mother feel.

"Yeah, well, take a good long look!" My father yelled sitting up on the floor. He leaned against the couch and dug in his front shirt pocket and pulled out a pack of cigarettes. "You just like me, boy." He chuckled.

"I could never be like you, my nigga. My wife loves me. I will never treat her the way you did ma." I yelled wiping the tear that dropped from my eye away roughly.

"Think again, youngin'." He sniffed. "You the spitting image of me. I bet if I ask your little wife right now she would have a different story." He removed the cigarette from the pack and continued to laugh.

I just glared at him. What had me the angriest was that he was telling the truth. Lately I felt like I had been acting more and more like him every day. I mean my wife didn't even come home because of how I treated her so who was I to talk?

"You know what, fuck you." I pointed at him. "Stay out my life! You dead to me." I yelled and bolted out the front door.

CHAPTER NINETEEN

TAE

I had been away from home without Bronco knowing where I was. I've never stayed out all night, much less for two days and I was scared at how he would react when it was finally time for us to communicate.

I had no idea what I was going to walk into when I got home. Would Bronco be mad at me? Did he even miss me? Thinking about how this would end had my stomach flipping.

The good thing was he should be at work now so I had time to at least take a bath and get ready for whatever he threw my way later.

When I walked inside the apartment I noticed the security alarm wasn't on. When I closed the door and looked around more I saw Bronco's duffle bag sitting on the floor.

By KEESHIA K.

He never went to work without that duffle. He must have taken the day off. I hoped he wasn't sick.

Concerned, I put my purse down on the dining room table and walked into our bedroom. I pushed the door slightly and it made a creaking sound slowly opening. And there he was, sitting on the edge of our bed in his work uniform with what looked like blood all over it.

"Bronco!" I yelled rushing into the room toward him. "What happened to you…Why…Why are you bleeding?" I asked afraid of the answer he would tell me.

He didn't say a word. He lifted his head slowly to look at me and huge tears fell from his eyes.

"Bronco…Talk to me, baby. Are you hurt?" I asked wanting to make sure he didn't need to go to the hospital.

He shook his head no. "She's gone, Tae." He said in a low voice.

"Who's gone?"

"My mama. She...She...killed herself." He broke down crying. "My mother's gone, and I can't...I can't deal with this shit."

I was speechless. I felt like someone sucked all the oxygen out of my body. Did he just tell me that his mother was dead because she killed herself? "Bronco, did you find her?" I asked trying to still figure out where the blood on him came from.

He nodded his head while balling uncontrollably.

I have never seen Bronco like this. I felt so sorry for him. He's devastated and I don't know all the details or why his mother did what she did, but I knew she was an unhappy woman. I hope now at least she has found her peace.

I kicked off my shoes and crawled on the bed behind him. I grabbed him in my arms and rocked him slowly. "It's ok, baby." I squeezed him as hard as I could. "Just let it out...I'm here."

By KEESHIA K.

He turned his body toward me and grabbed me. He continued to cry as he held onto me. I'm so glad I was here. I wondered if I could feel his energy, which is why I decided I had to come home today.

After Bronco settled down, I realized I needed to take care of home. So I drew Bronco a bubble bath and got him undressed. While he soaked in the tub I cleaned up the bedroom and changed the sheets on the bed. There was nothing better than being clean and then getting into a clean bed. Especially when you're in pain.

Once he was out of the tub and settled in, I cooked him his favorite comfort meal, split pea soup and a couple of grilled turkey and cheese sandwiches. Although he didn't have an appetite he could never resist this meal and I knew he needed to eat something.

I wanted to lift his spirits as much as I could anyway, given the circumstances.

"Baby, is your dad gonna make the arrangements for the funeral? Or will there even be a funeral?" I asked sitting on the bed as I watched Bronco force his soup down.

"We got any beer?" He replied ignoring my question. I guess he didn't want to talk about this yet.

"Yes," I said. I walked out the room to grab him one out the fridge. I have no idea how we will get through this. He has never been close to his father but now when I mentioned his name I noticed his jaw clinched.

I grabbed two beers and opened one taking a huge gulp out of the bottle. I realized I hadn't eaten anything yet, but I really needed this drink.

When I got back to the bedroom I handed the unopened beer to Bronco. He took it from me, opened it and downed the whole thing in one gulp. I watched in amazement as I continued to sip mine.

184 **By KEESHIA K.**

"Come here." He said putting the empty bottle down on the bedside table.

I walked over to the side of the bed and stood near him. He reached up and started to pull me down onto him. I slammed my beer on the table quickly so I wouldn't spill it on the bed as he placed me on top of his body and kissed me.

I kissed him back but when I felt his dick getting hard I pulled away from him. "Bronco, stop." I told him not wanting to take the kiss further. "Not now, not like this."

"Come on, baby, please. I need to feel you. I need to be inside of you. Please don't do me like this." He begged me.

"Bronco, I have been gone for days." I explained. "We have a lot to talk about and until then I'm just not comfortable having sex with you. I need more time and I know that hurts you but I need to be honest."

"Time...Time for what?" He sat up and yelled. I got up and straightened my clothes. "You my wife and I need you right now." He pointed at the floor. "I mean, how the fuck time gonna change that?"

"I'm not sure." I told him honestly. "I know you hurting, but I just can't do that right now. I'm sorry."

"You know what, if you can't be here for me when I need you most then fuck it, I'll get somebody in here who will." He yelled. "It ain't like you haven't been out doing your thing anyway."

"You know what...I don't need this." I said. I walked to my closet and grabbed my pink duffle bag and began packing clothes into it. "Nothing changes with you which is why nothing changes in our relationship."

"Hold up...What you doing?" He asked jumping up out the bed. "You can't go nowhere...Please don't...Don't do this."

"I'm leaving, Bronco. I'm trying to be here for you right now but I won't be taken advantage of anymore. I

By KEESHIA K.

refuse to end up like your mother." I said realizing that may have been harsh but it was the truth. I continued packing.

He took a deep breath. "Tae, I'm sorry. And you right." He shrugged. "You know I ain't mean it, you know what I'm saying. I just want you; I just need to feel good right now. Please…Don't go." He pleaded.

"I'm sorry. I can't do that." I zipped up my bag. "Goodbye, Bronco." I picked up my duffle and walked out the apartment.

CHAPTER TWENTY

TAE

I don't know why I was so nervous. It was probably because of the way Siena blew up at me when I wanted to answer Bronco's call. I wasn't expecting her to be that angry.

So I may be stupid for even going back there, but she did offer to let me stay and at the moment I really needed her. Besides, Bronco was too heavy for me and I needed a breath of fresh air until I could figure some things out.

I took a deep breath. I sat my duffle bag down on her stoop and knocked on her door gently. I didn't even call first to see if she was home which was kinda fucked up because I wouldn't want nobody popping up on me.

The more I stood there thinking about it, the more I felt crazy for even being there. When I came to my senses, I picked up my bag and turned around to leave.

By KEESHIA K.

I didn't know exactly where I was gonna go but I knew it couldn't be my parent's house. Too many questions would be asked that I didn't have the answers to right now.

"Taevonne?" Siena called out my name from behind me. I turned around and faced her. "I didn't hear the door. Were you out here long?" She asked looking at me.

I stood there for a brief moment and weighed my options, until I realized I didn't have many. There was no way I was going back home. Not right now anyway.

"Oh, hey, Siena." I smiled although I felt dumb. "Look, I'm so sorry for just barging up on you like this but I...well earlier you offered to—"

"I'm so glad you came back." She smiled. "I mean I acted like a complete lame. I'm so sorry for blanking out like that, Tae. You did nothing to deserve any of it." She said shocking me. "I hope you can forgive me. Do you?"

"Don't even think about it," I waved the air. "And thank you for apologizing." I said feeling a little better about my predicament. "Ummm…Were you serious about me staying with you for—"

"Oh my God, yes!" She yelled excitedly cutting me off. She ran off her stoop and grabbed me up in a huge hug before kissing me on my lips. "My home is open to you now and always!"

The kiss was a little strange, especially since she was bare foot and we were outside standing in front of her place and not in her bedroom. I mean she acted like I just came home from combat. I smiled awkwardly. "Well, thank you." I cleared my throat. "Um…can we go—"

"Yes, of course. Get in here." She locked her arm around mine and walked me inside her place.

By KEESHIA K.

It was later in the evening and I had my phone on airplane mode. I'm not sure if Bronco tried to call me or not but I wasn't feeling him right now so it didn't matter. I really wanted to be there when he needed me but too much pain caused me to harden up.

I know it may be a bad look not being at his side now with his mom's death and all, but I can't be in a bad situation mentally or sexually. We need this time apart to sort our marriage out. Shit was very rocky in our house; and I couldn't deal with him let alone his grief too.

Besides, I was really enjoying staying with Siena. She was everything I felt like I needed at the time. She was warm, compassionate, smart, funny, sexy and very welcoming.

As soon as she brought me inside her apartment I told her what happened between Bronco and I, when I got home. She was saddened to hear about his mother dying and even cried with me. After we shed a lot of tears she drew *me* a bubble bath and washed and massaged my body. I felt like I was away at a spa and I needed each and every touch.

When she was done she even made me a delicious dinner and I thought I was a good cook. Her meal was so perfect. She made garlic mashed potatoes with rosemary chicken breasts and asparagus. To be honest I had never tasted anything so good.

We had just finished dinner and was sitting at her table listening to Drake's latest, *Nice For What*, blasting throughout her living room.

"Siena, I just wanted to say thank you again. I mean, I don't know what I did to deserve you but I'm grateful."

She picked up the speaker remote and turned the music down. "Tae, you don't have to thank me anymore. You've done it a million times already. Like I said I love having you." She walked towards me and straddled me in the chair. With her arms resting on my shoulder she smiled. "Consider my place, yours." She bent down and kissed me deeply which made my pussy jump.

Slowly she pulled her lips off mine and stared into my eyes. "What?" I asked smiling.

"I'm going to do everything in my power to make you happy, Taevonne. Now that you're mine, you will never want for or need anything. We'll be so happy together, trust me." She said before she leaned in again for a kiss. Except this time I didn't kiss back. Instead of getting off my lap, she continued to look at me with a huge smile.

"Siena, umm…What do you mean I'm your's?" I looked at her. "I, I didn't understand what you just meant."

Her smile washed off her face. "I mean, you mine." She kissed my forehead and it irritated me. "My girlfriend, since we live together now. I mean, are you confused?"

I sat up straighter in the chair. I wanted to stand up but she didn't budge off my lap. I remembered how upset she got earlier and chose my words carefully. Now I realized it was definitely a mistake coming back over.

"Siena, please don't get me wrong, I'm very grateful for you allowing me to stay here. But, by doing so I'm not committing to being in a relationship with you. I'm still married. You understand that right?"

"Why the fuck do you keep bringing up that you're married?" She asked leaping up off my lap, finally. "I'm so sick of hearing that dumb shit! I mean it ain't like them vows sacred."

"Because I *am* married!" I yelled back. "Siena, I know we have a good time and all sexually but I could never be with you on a solo basis." I told her feeling shocked at her reaction.

"So you just toying with me then?" She crossed her arms over her chest. "You just playing house with me and after I lick all your wounds clean you just gonna run right back home to that motherless bastard?" She screamed while standing over me.

I was so nervous at what was happening now that I could hear my own heartbeat in my ears. For some reason I felt like my life was in danger and I could honestly say I had never felt like that before.

I stood up slowly. "I think I may have given you the wrong impression about you and I." I told her. "And if I have, I'm so sorry."

She glared at me for what seemed like forever before she spoke. "You know what, Tae you are a selfish bitch. Just get out my house!" She paused. "I'm sick of looking at you anyway."

I walked down the hallway and into the bedroom where my bag was near the closet door. I had on sweatpants and a T-shirt and was looking for my flip-flops until I remembered they were in the living room. Anything else I had there I was willing to part ways with because I needed to get out of this place immediately. While I was still alive.

As I gathered my things I heard dishes crashing into the sink in the kitchen and knew Siena was on one, again. I snatched my purse off the dresser and headed to the front door.

"I can't believe after everything we shared you would just leave me!" Siena stood in front of me blocking my steps. This woman was insane. Didn't she just put me out three minutes ago?

"I need to go, Siena. I'll call you in a few days once things have calmed down." I said as I sidestepped around her.

"No, you won't!" She yelled behind me. As I reached for the doorknob I felt something slam against my head. And just like that I was light on my feet like I was floating before everything suddenly went black.

Damn!

By KEESHIA K.

CHAPTER TWENTY-ONE
BRONCO

I had been calling Tae all day and night and she wouldn't answer my calls. What the entire fuck was happening in my life right now? I mean shit had never been so off with me.

I ain't fuck with my pops no more and although he kept calling me about the service for my mama, I been ignoring him. I ain't 'bout to go to the fake ass memorial service he was having. Why should I go? My moms not gonna be there and them shits be for everybody else anyway.

Plus if I do step up in there and witness the shit show my pops gonna put on, I may choke the fake out his ass and get locked up. Nah, it was best that I kept my distance.

Besides, I needed to get my whole life together like now or I wasn't gonna make it man. It's like I had zero support system. I haven't seen or heard from my wife in over twenty-four hours. And she don't seem to give a fuck neither.

I know she heated with me, but I gotta talk to her. I need to make this shit square before I lose her for good. To be honest before she agreed to my shit I never thought it was possible. I just took my shot at what I wanted but now I knew that I was completely wrong.

We had only been married a few months and I would have never thought we'd end up like this. I had no business carrying shit the way that I did with her and now karma got me by the balls.

I needed to keep trying to work shit out so I called Tae's phone again. This time it went straight to her voicemail no ringing. When it beeped I decided to leave her a message, which I hadn't been doing.

"Tae, baby, it's B...Look, I'm sorry for being a savage. You ain't never deserved none of the shit I put on you. I can't even believe I made you go through with that on our wedding day." I paused looking out my car window at nothing in particular. "Dealing with my moms being gone really put a lot of shit in

By KEESHIA K.

perspective for me and I realized how bad I been fucking up. Just…Just come home. I promise it'll be different and we can work this out, baby…Please. Don't leave me. I love you."

I ended my message. I just prayed that she would forgive me and that it wasn't too late.

I walked into the bar where I was meeting up with Randy and Quentin from my job. They heard about my mama passing and made me come out to grab some drinks. I told them naw at first but since Tae wasn't at home, what was the use of being there?

"Sup, fellas." I said walking up to them. They were both seated at the bar with an empty stool between them.

"Hey, Bronco." Randy stood up and gave me a one armed embrace. "Sorry again about your moms." He said to me before sitting back down.

"Thanks, Randy, man." I told him.

Quentin didn't get up but nudged the empty stool in the middle for me to sit down. "What you drinking? It's on me." He said.

I pulled out the stool and took a seat. "I'll take a double of Gentleman's Jack, no rocks." I told the bartender. She looked at me suspiciously but took my order.

"How you been holding on, Bronco?" Quentin asked taking a sip from his drink.

I shrugged my shoulders. "Barely, man...Barely. I just been sitting in the house trying to figure all this shit out." I told them.

"What about the service?" He paused. "Is there anything you, Tae or your dad need? I can help." Quentin offered.

By KEESHIA K.

"Oh, yeah, me too." Randy chimed in. "My uncle drives for a funeral home on Kennedy Street. I can talk to him about using their services if you need. Just say the word."

"Naw, ya'll, I appreciate the offers, but my pops is handling that end and I'm not getting involved. Me and that dude ain't seeing eye to eye right now anyway." I told them. "I really don't want to talk about his ass...ever."

"I ain't sure what's up with you and your father, man but now ain't the time for ya'll to fall apart. You need each other." Randy told me. "If you can put your differences aside, do that now. Life too short."

I just looked at him as my nose flared. "I don't need that nigga. Not now and not in the future so leave it be." I told him. He threw his hands up like he was surrendering.

"How's Tae doing?" Quentin asked.

"Shit, truth be told…I wish I knew." I confessed. "We got into it the other day and she packed some things and left. She won't even answer my calls. It's like everything bad that *can* happen *is* happening."

The bartender came back and placed my drink in front of me. "Thank you." I told her and picked it up to take a sip.

"What you do now, nigga?" Quentin asked. "I hate to do it to you since you grieving but I gotta know."

"Man, it's a long story, but bottom line is you were right. I asked too much of her with that open marriage shit and now I gotta do whatever it takes to try and get her back."

"Look, dog. I don't really know what's going on with ya'll but Tae loves you, Bronco. I mean that's evident otherwise she would have told your ass off when you came at her with that shit in the beginning." Randy said. "So, just get back to why she fell in love with you in the first place and she'll come around."

I nodded my head hoping that what Randy said rang true although deep down I knew it didn't.

"Get the fuck outta here with that love sick shit, Randy." Quentin said. "You don't know the first thing 'bout women." He continued sipping his drink. "Over there giving advice and shit."

"So what you think I should do?" I asked Quentin.

"Personally, I think that it may be too late. I think that you had an opportunity to turn this around before it got out of hand and you didn't and now she may be gone for good." Quentin said fucking my head up even more.

I grabbed my drink off the bar and threw it down my throat with anger. "Scuse me, can I get another?" I asked the bartender.

Instead of getting my drink she asked if she could talk to me in private. I nodded and got up from the bar while Quentin and Randy looked at me surprised. We walked down to the other end of the bar where there was no one around. I was curious as to what she wanted.

"I'm sorry to pull you from your friends but there's something I think you should know and I didn't want to say it around them." I nodded my head curiously. "The last time you were in here I saw you with your wife and another chick named Siena." She started. She really had my attention now. "Well you need to stay far away from her, she's dangerous." She warned me. "I'm talking about Siena of course."

"Dangerous, how?" I asked feeling nauseous thinking about Tae being harmed.

"I used to live in her apartment building and let's just say I've seen and heard all kinds of things about that chick. She's crazy and not to be trusted." She paused. "If I were you and your wife I would stay far away from Siena before it's too late."

I felt like I was about to shit in my Levi's. I had to find my wife.

By KEESHIA K.

CHAPTER TWENTY-TWO

TAE

Siena was off her nut. She knocked me out with a blow to the head when I was trying to leave. Now she had me tied up to her dining room chair where she held a gun on me. I can't believe I wasn't more careful with this woman. What was I thinking?

"You think your shit don't stink don't you?" Siena asked as she looked down at me from the barrel of her 9mm.

"Siena, I have no idea what you mean." I told her confused at what she was talking about. I feared for my life. "All I want to do is go home. Let me out and I promise not to say a word."

She looked like she wanted to shoot me in the face. "Don't play dumb with me, Taevonne." She paused. "You led me on to think what we had was real and then you trivialized it like your shit don't stink. That's what the fuck I mean." She stated. "And you need to realize it."

I took several deep breaths to try and calm my nerves because I felt a panic attack coming up on me. "Siena, I'm being honest with you. I think you are a very attractive and sexy woman and being with you has given me so much confidence." I smiled at her but it felt fake. "You have shown me things I didn't even know were capable with my body sexually and I will always be grateful to you for that. But, I could never be in a relationship with you. I'm just not gay, I never was. I just did that for my husband." I explained. "But it doesn't mean I didn't enjoy our time together."

She looked like she wanted to cry as she paced back and fourth in front of me. This woman is real live crazy. *I need to get myself out of here.* I thought as I wiggled my hands while she wasn't looking at me to try and free them.

"So basically, you used me." She paused. "You and your little husband used me in your marital bedroom games and now you trying to throw me away?" She asked. "You might as well be honest."

　　　　By KEESHIA K.

"No!" I yelled. "That's not it at all. I'm so sorry if you feel like that, but I thought Bronco and I were always clear with you about what we wanted. I mean you acted like you were with it before so what changed?" I asked.

"Love!" She yelled at me. She picked up the TV remote control and hurled it at my head. I ducked before it connected with my face. This psycho loved throwing shit. "Love changed. I fell in love with you the first moment I saw you behind that counter at your job." She said wiping the tears that started to flow from her eyes. "I never wanted him. It was always about you."

I couldn't believe what I was hearing. She sounded like some lovesick cheerleader. She was far from the strong woman I thought she was. I wished I never said anything to her back then but now it was all too late.

She stood in front of me as if she was waiting for me to tell her something. But I didn't say a word. I just looked up at her with pleading eyes.

"Wow...So I tell you that I'm in love with you and you sit there like you taking a shit?" She said with her wild eyes peering into mine.

"Siena, I don't know what you want me to say to you." I replied. "I'm very fond of you and I'm grateful that you have been there for me during all of this." I shrugged. "But I don't love you. I never have."

Siena walked over to me and smacked me across the face with the gun. I felt my right eye open up and blood flowed out from the wound. What the fuck did I say that shit for? The look in her eyes told me that she was about to end my life. Maybe I should have lied and told her I loved her. At least it might have bought me some time. Now I was fucked.

"You a stupid bitch!" She yelled. "You know what...Maybe I should do to you what I did to my ex-girlfriend. Maybe that'll teach you to love me back." She said before she stormed off into the kitchen.

What did that mean? I always knew her story about her ex didn't add up but now I was really concerned. While she was gone I worked feverishly to

By KEESHIA K.

get my hands untied. I felt the string getting looser but not enough to work my hands out. I needed a miracle.

"Yeah...Bitches like you only know one thing...Pain." Siena said as she walked back into the living room and up in front of me. Her gun was now tucked into her waist and she held a knife.

"Siena, what did you do to your ex-girlfriend?" I asked, hoping it would buy me some time. "Can you talk to me?"

She dropped her arms to the side of her body and tilted her head sideways as if she were trying to see through me. Then she smiled.

"Didn't I tell you? She tried to leave me too. I had given her the best year of my life and when she decided she was done she wanted to leave." She told me with crazed eyes. "No one leaves me! So I stopped her."

"You...You killed her?"

"I crept up on her at night when she was on the way into her apartment. After she just finished fucking her basic bitch, I stabbed her in the stomach. I watched her die right there on the sidewalk." She confessed.

This was worse than I thought and I was terrified. "But I'm not like her, Siena." I pleaded. "She was your girlfriend but you and I are different."

"It's the same thing! She tried to play me too. Would call me and run to me when she had problems at home and after I put her back together she would abandon me again. Just like what Bronco does to you. Don't you see?" She asked before she climbed on my lap straddling me again. "We're the same, baby. It's just too bad you don't love me either." She kissed me on my lips that were soaked with my own blood. "Goodbye, Taevonne."

She lifted the knife to stab me but I had gotten my hands free and jumped to my feet with my hands clasped around her throat. I tried with all the strength I could find to choke the life out of her but while she struggled to get out of my grip she was able to still poke at my body with the knife.

210   *By KEESHIA K.*

I didn't let that stop me because I knew if I let go of my hold on her throat I would be dead. I continued to grip her neck tighter and tighter until I saw that her eyes went from dark and crazed to blank and motionless.

Suddenly I felt lightheaded. I rolled off Siena and heard a loud crash before I blacked out.

BRONCO

"Tae!!!" I yelled when I saw my bloodied and beaten wife passed out on the floor. "I'm here, baby. I'm here." I shouted as I rushed up to her. "Hold on, Tae. I'm getting you some help. Stay with me."

I scooped her fragile body up off the floor and dipped out the apartment. Based on how it looked inside, Siena had Tae tied up but she must've gotten free and tried to kill her.

I don't know if Siena was dead or not and I don't give a fuck. My only focus was to get Tae to the emergency room.

I placed her inside the back seat of my truck and jumped behind the wheel. "Tae, baby, I'm gonna get you to the hospital. Just keep fighting! Keep fighting." I yelled as I silently prayed that I wasn't too late.

By KEESHIA K.

CHAPTER TWENTY-THREE
BRONCO

You know, I never was the praying type of nigga but after I saw my wife lying in her own blood struggling to stay in this world, I had to start. I begged whatever God was supposed to watch over us to please not take her from me and it worked. Tae was in the hospital and she was still breathing.

I sat in her hospital room where I had been for the last two days. I ain't wanna leave her side.

Tae got stabbed in her chest and shoulder four times and although she lost a lot of blood, she took it like a G. I can't say the same for ole girl though. Tae choked her to death. The police came through here and tried to press us about what went down. I told 'em what I could but Tae hasn't been coherent enough to talk to 'em yet. And I'm glad too. She shouldn't have to do their jobs.

"Bronco," Tae opened her eyes and called my name. I jumped up out the chair and rushed to her side.

"I'm here, baby. How you feel?" I asked relieved she was finally awake. I stood over her and reached out to grab her hand.

She closed her eyes and tried to adjust her position in the bed. She took a deep breath and winced. "It hurts to breathe."

"I bet, let me get the nurse." I told her. I pushed the button attached to her bed with the nurse's picture on it.

A minute later the nurse came in. "Well now, look who's awake." She said as she walked into the room and checked Tae's vitals.

"My mouth is dry. And it hurts when I breathe in." Tae told her. She looked like she was hurting bad. "I...I never been in so much pain in all of my life."

By KEESHIA K.

"You are very lucky to be here Mrs. Lawson. You sustained several life threatening stab wounds but you were lucky enough to get to the ER on time too." The nurse continued. "We'll get you some more pain meds and some ice water. You can eat the ice chips and sip the water slow."

Tae nodded and looked up at me after the nurse left out the room. "Bronco, what happened? I don't remember how I got here." She asked me.

I pulled my chair up close to her bedside and sat down. I reached over and grabbed her hand carefully. "Baby, you were at Siena's spot and it looked like she was holding you hostage cuz you had rope on your wrist." I explained. "I found out where she lived and came to get you. I knocked and when I heard what sounded like somebody rumbling in the apartment I broke down the door."

Her eyes bugged open as I ran down what happened. "The last thing I remember was sitting in her living room tied to a chair. She had a gun on me." Tears began to flow from her eyes. "I was so scared."

"Yeah, the cops said she had a gun in her waist when they found her too." I told her. "That bitch was psycho."

"Found her?" She said. "Bronco, is Siena…is she…"

"Yeah, baby. She gone." I had to tell her. She closed her eyes and more tears streamed down the sides of her cheeks.

The nurse came in again with a Styrofoam cup of ice water. She handed it to me and walked back out of the room. I sat the cup down on the tray.

I stood up. "Look, Tae, you can't feel bad about that. Siena was troubled, baby. She had a mental health history. She was unstable and if you didn't get yourself free and fight her she would have killed you." I explained.

She sniffled and slowly lifted her hand to wipe her tears away. "How did you know where she lived?" She asked me.

By KEESHIA K.

"Baby, that's a long story, and I'll tell you all of it later. I just want you to rest up and get better. I lost my mind when I came in there and found you. I thought I lost you, Tae. I've never been so scared in all my life." I confessed.

A small smile appeared on her face. "I'm sorry, Bronco. I should have never left. I..." She began to cough. "I..."

I reached over and grabbed the water cup and placed it near her mouth and positioned the straw by her lips. She took a sip. "That better?" I asked.

She nodded.

"Baby, don't talk. Just hear me out, please?"

She nodded again. "Okay."

"I was bugging asking you to do that bamma shit," I said to her. "If I ain't come at you like that you wouldn't have gotten hurt or even be in this position. I know all this shit my fault and I wanna make it right baby." I told her.

"Make it right?" She questioned in a low whisper.

"Yeah, I feel like our whole marriage was set up for failure because of how it started out and we never gonna be right unless something changes. So I wanna do it over. I want you to marry me again, but this time no ultimatum and no clauses." I told her.

I held her hand and waited for her response. It seemed like an eternity passed by while I waited.

She closed her eyes and nodded her head slowly. That's all the answer I needed.

"Bae, I promise," I said confidently. "I will love you and protect you with all that I am. No more cheating…no other women. Just you and me as it should be. I love you, Tae." I told her. A tear snuck out my eye.

"I love you too, Bronco." She whispered. "Thank you for saving my life. I will forever be grateful to you for that."

By KEESHIA K.

I bent down and kissed her lips softly. "You can thank me by getting some rest and getting better. I need you at full strength for our wedding reception's dance break. We gotta hit the *Kid N Play*."

She laughed and then screwed up her face. "Don't make me laugh." She said.

I smiled. Seeing her laugh warmed my heart. But seeing her alive made me want to fight for our marriage. I'm grateful I got a second chance and I promised on my eyes, I wouldn't fuck it up again.

CHAPTER TWENTY-FOUR

BRONCO

It felt good to get back to normal. It seemed like everything that could go wrong over the last few weeks did go wrong. Tae was still recovering and I was back at work. I had been out ever since my mom died. Although being at work felt like my life was getting back on track, everything had changed.

"Bronco, I need to speak with you in my office." Alicia stood in the doorway of the garage and looked at me closely. Her arms were crossed tightly over her chest.

"I'll be right there." I told her. I put my wrench down and grabbed the rag off the toolbox. After I wiped my hands I removed the purple latex gloves I always wore and tossed them on the car.

I'm not sure what Alicia wanted but it probably had something to do with the loss of my mama. They normally gave some type of cards or flower

By KEESHIA K.

arrangements at work when somebody had a death in the family. Although it would be nice for real I could do without all the mushy shit. I preferred to deal with my stuff on my own.

I approached Alicia's office and knocked lightly on the door. "Come in, Bronco and please close the door behind you."

"What's up, Alicia?" I asked as I pulled out the chair in front of her desk to take a seat. "Everything okay?" I didn't see a card, flowers or anything else.

"Please, keep standing, this won't take long." She told me.

I pushed the seat back to its original position and looked at my boss.

"We were all very sorry to hear about your mother, Bronco." She paused." Did you receive the flowers we sent?"

"Uh, yeah, I got 'em. Thank you." I told her just remembering that I did get a delivery at my apartment of flowers but when Tae got attacked it slipped my mind. "Me and my family appreciated—"

"Good." She cut me off. "Well, as you know when an employee has a death in the family they receive time off with pay for three days. Since you reported your mother's death and up until today when you officially returned to work, it has been seven days that you have been off." She said.

"I know I only got three days but I was the one who actually found my mother and it kinda fucked...I mean messed me up so, uh, I was just trying to pull myself together before I came back to work." I explained.

"Bronco, although I understand your situation and sympathize with you, the company does not allow for no calls and no shows. So unfortunately I have to let you go. I'm sorry."

"What? Let me go?" I asked thrown completely the fuck off. "You mean to tell me that my mother died and because I needed a few more days to deal I get fired?" I frowned. "How that sound?"

By KEESHIA K.

"Bronco, you can't take off for days on end without contacting your job. We have a business to run and had to compensate by having other mechanics work overtime. Your antics caused us more in payroll." Alicia said.

"My antics!" I yelled heated. "You act like I went to the Bahamas or some shit! My mother died." I explained.

"I know, and again we are very sorry for your loss but we cannot keep you on as an employee here. Now please, clear out your locker and leave the premises. Your last paycheck will be direct deposited into your account on Friday."

I was in shock. Part of me wanted to jump across her desk and choke the shit out of her. But I knew I wasn't trying to add a record and jail time on top of being fired. I took a deep breath and tried a different approach.

"Alicia, I really need my job." I paused. "Ever since I got married I have been going about my life in a selfish manner. Now I have the opportunity to turn that around and fix what I messed up. But that can't happen without working. Please, can you give me another chance?" I begged.

"Mr. Lawson, I have already told you to leave. If you are not gone within the next three minutes I will call security to escort you out."

I drove down the street on my way home fucked up. I felt like something was off. I mean I know what Alicia said about why I was fired but that didn't add up. I needed answers so I decided to call Quentin. I knew he would know what it was really hittin' for and give it to me straight.

I grabbed my cell phone out of my duffle bag and connected it to my truck. Once it was hooked up I tapped the phone icon next to Quentin's name to call him.

"Hello," Quentin said after two rings.

"Quentin, what's up, slim? Why the fuck did Alicia just fire me?" I asked. I wanted to get right down to it. "She tripping like shit."

"Look, Bronco, man, I don't know no more than you do." He paused. "What did she tell you was the reason?" He asked.

"Nigga, stop bullshitting with me." I turned onto the highway. "I know you know what's up." I was angry because he was faking dumb. Him and the boss were cool and everybody knew it.

He took a deep breath. "Aight, she heard what went down with Tae and knew what happened to her was because of you." He sighed. "So, she used the extra days you were gone as an excuse to axe you." He explained.

I frowned. "Hold up…How the fuck she know 'bout all that in the first place?" I asked.

"I told her."

"What?" I yelled. I had to pull over because I felt like I was about to crash. "Fuck you mean you told her?" I was completely confused.

"Look, man…She pulled me in the office and asked where you were and why hadn't you come back to work or called." He paused. "So I told her what happened to Tae."

"Why the fuck would you tell her that shit, Quentin? You know that bitch already don't fuck with me. That was all the excuse she needed!" I yelled.

"Look, nigga, I thought I was helping you. But truth be told had you been more of a man your wife wouldn't have gotten hurt and you would still have your job." He yelled back before ending the call.

I needed to think of something quick. If Tae finds this shit out not only will she not wanna re-marry me

226   *By KEESHIA K.*

she might not wanna have nothing to do with me since I won't be able to take care of her while she recovered. Fuck!

I knocked on my father's door. I hadn't been anywhere near his house since the day they carried my mama's body out of it but it was time. I needed help and I felt like this nigga owed me.

The door opened slowly and my father appeared in the doorway. He looked bad. Worse than I had ever seen him. His cheeks were sunken in like he hadn't eaten in a week and his beard was scraggly. He had a Capone dangling from his lip and a glass of something dark in his hand.

"What you doing here, Bronco? I thought I was dead to you." He said as he blocked my entrance.

"I need to talk to you." I told him looking down before I looked into his eyes again. He opened the door wider and let me inside.

"So, talk." He said as he closed the door behind me while he stood next to it. He placed the glass on the table by the door.

"Tae got hurt a little while ago and I got fired today because I was off work too long tending to her." He didn't even look at me while I talked. "So, I need to borrow some money to cover this wedding and take care of her until I get another job." I asked. "I figure it's the least you can do seeing as how you killed my mother and all."

He chuckled lightly and dropped the ashes from the Capone into his hand. "I never used to smoke in the house. Your mother would get upset if I did, said the smoke got into the drapes and made the house stink. She didn't want it smelly when company came over." He rambled. "What I wouldn't give for her to get after me for smoking in here now."

By KEESHIA K.

I clenched my jaw and swallowed the lump that formed in my throat. "So what's up, pop, you gonna loan me the money or not?" I asked angry that he made me feel sorry for him missing my mother.

He looked up at me and I saw a tear roll down his cheek. "I'm sorry for how I treated your mother. She didn't deserve it." He said before he turned around and grabbed his checkbook off the table and started writing in it.

I rolled my eyes at him and looked around the house. It was dark and quiet and felt cold. There were several bouquets of flowers all over the living room. They must have come from the funeral service. I started feeling uneasy being back there like I could feel all the pain my moms must have felt.

I tried to shake off what I was feeling and looked back at my father. He handed me a check for ten thousand dollars.

My eyes widened. "Pop, that's way more than I can payback. I—"

"Don't worry about it, Bronco. Just take care of your wife better than I did mine. The men in our family ain't fit to be alone." He said looking at me sadly. "I really did love her you know?" He said before he grabbed his drink off the table and walked up the steps and into his bedroom.

I wiped my hand down my face roughly and took a deep breath. I took another look at the check and shook my head.

With this check, I knew I would be able to take care of Tae and pay for this wedding 2.0. But, to do it right I was gonna need help.

I pulled my cell phone out of my pocket and called Tae's best friend Stacy.

"Bronco, this you…What the T?" She asked in her usual colorful fashion.

"Yeah, Stacy it's me. Look, I wanna renew my vows with Tae. Well, not even renew but fix my mistake. I know you know the details of our first wedding and what I did so I'm trying to set shit right and I need your help. You in?" I asked.

"Honey, I thought you'd never ask!"

CHAPTER TWENTY-FIVE

BRONCO

THREE MONTHS LATER

Reverend Miles looked at his watch and then up at me awkwardly as we stood at the alter. This was the same alter we stood at almost one year ago the first time I married Tae. But now I was the one up here sweating while I waited on her.

"I'm sure she's just running a little late." I said to him, as I hoped that was the case. "She's moving a lot slower these days." I smiled nervously. "Because of the accident and all." I lied. Not wanting him to know she was almost killed by a psychotic freak.

He nodded and smiled back. I looked past him and over at Stacy. She bugged her eyes out at me and shrugged her shoulders not knowing what the hold up was.

By KEESHIA K.

I took my pocket square out of my tuxedo jacket and wiped the beads of sweat off my forehead. *What I wouldn't give for a drink right now.* I thought as I tucked my hanky back into my jacket. Now I know what Tae must have felt like standing up here on our first wedding day.

I felt the heat from the small crowd of our families staring a hole in the back of my head. I reached inside my pants pocket and grabbed my cell phone. I hit the button to check and see if Tae had called or texted me.

When my phone lit up I saw I had a message from Tae and felt my heart sink down into the pit of my stomach.

When I opened the text and read it, a sly smile spread across my face and I felt a moment of relief. Tae's message said, **Come Outside**. There was a smiley face emoji next to it.

I chuckled and tucked my phone back into my pocket. As I turned around to walk out the church my pop approached me.

"Son, you want me to go find her?" He asked with a serious look spread over his face. He was doing a lot better since the weeks right after my mother's suicide. Although I could tell he still missed her deeply.

"Naw, I'm good, pop. I know just where she is and she's waiting on me. I'll be right back." I said as I jogged past him and headed out the church.

I figured she wanted me to take back the vows I made her give me of having another woman in the picture, before she said yes. And I was willing to do just that.

I pushed open the doors with a huge smile on my face in anticipation of seeing my beautiful bride. But when I looked out, Tae wasn't there. I walked out the door and down the steps to get a better look. Maybe she was on her way or about to pull up.

I jogged to the curb and looked up and down both sides of the street and didn't see her anywhere.

I was confused.

By KEESHIA K.

I decided to go and sit on the steps and wait on her. I mean she had to be coming or she wouldn't have texted me. Right?

Before I walked back, I looked around the street for a few moments but the anticipation was killing me. Maybe I missed her somehow and she was already inside.

When I turned to walk back towards the church I noticed something sitting on the bench that I didn't see when I first came out. I moved closer to get a better look. It was a box of Capone's and a folded piece of paper under them.

I grabbed the Capone's and picked up the paper and unfolded it. It was a note to me in Tae's handwriting that said:

ISSA NO FOR ME...IT'S OVER!

I dropped the note out my hand and flopped down on the bench.

Damn!

EPILOGUE
BRONCO

TWO MONTHS LATER

I started a new job last week. It was at another car dealership service garage but the pay and benefits were almost the same.

I liked being there because after Tae left me stuck at the alter, I felt like I needed a whole new start. The people were cool for the most part. There was a few mechanics that worked with me now that knew some nigga's I used to work with at my old job. So I didn't escape it completely but what could I do the city was small.

I hadn't seen or heard from Tae since the night before my remix wedding day. When I picked myself up from embarrassment and went back to our apartment after she left me at the church I found all of her things were gone. She planned on leaving me all

By KEESHIA K.

along and I didn't see it coming. In my mind she always loved me so why would that change?

She waited until I left the apartment the night before the wedding and packed her shit to leave me. I'm sure she knew what she was gonna do and even though some people may think I deserved it I felt like she could've done it a better way.

She changed her number and hadn't once reached out to me. I heard through some of the mechanic's I used to work with that she got a new nigga or whatever. Apparently, her and this dude even rented some house and moved in together.

It took me a minute and a few bucks but I got the address to their little place and decided to roll through there. I mean I know I did her dirty but who hadn't made a mistake or two here and there? And when I played the tapes back she may not have liked it in the beginning but after some time she was enjoying the women too. I know it.

I felt at the very least she owed me the decency of looking in my face and telling me she was done and that's exactly what I planned to get.

When I pulled up in front of the house, I saw a familiar looking truck parked in the driveway. I would know this truck anywhere because of the personal touches the nigga put on it. So the moment I saw it, I felt my blood start to boil.

I parked my truck and jumped out to get a closer look since it was dark outside which made it hard for me to be seen clearly.

I crept up closer to the house and saw two figures inside the living room through the window. The curtains were wide open and they looked to be watching something on TV.

As I made my way closer the couple became more and more recognizable. I saw Tae but it was who was hugged up under her that made my jaw twitch.

I looked on in anger as I saw Quentin and Tae laughing together on the couch. He leaned in and

238   *By KEESHIA K.*

kissed her passionately on the lips and I felt my stomach flip.

I realized how I must have looked like a creep standing by the window so I looked around to make sure no one was watching me. Then I took off and headed back toward my truck.

I jumped inside and closed the truck door. "Shit!" I yelled as I punched the steering wheel. "He must think I'ma lame!" I said out loud to myself.

All this time he was telling me how much I shouldn't do that threesome shit with Tae and how it could come back to bite me and here he was sliding in on her left.

"Oh ain't no way in hell I'ma let that nigga ride off into the sunset with my wife! I'ma be on a mission to make sure they both get what's coming to 'em! That's my word!" I yelled to myself. I cut my eyes towards the house for one last look before I started my truck and sped off down the block.

Now it was time to come up with a plan.

GAY FOR MY BAE   239

The Cartel Publications Order Form

www.thecartelpublications.com

Inmates **ONLY** receive novels for $10.00 per book **PLUS** shipping fee **PER BOOK.**

(Mail Order **MUST** come from inmate directly to receive discount)

Shyt List 1	_____	$15.00
Shyt List 2	_____	$15.00
Shyt List 3	_____	$15.00
Shyt List 4	_____	$15.00
Shyt List 5	_____	$15.00
Pitbulls In A Skirt	_____	$15.00
Pitbulls In A Skirt 2	_____	$15.00
Pitbulls In A Skirt 3	_____	$15.00
Pitbulls In A Skirt 4	_____	$15.00
Pitbulls In A Skirt 5	_____	$15.00
Victoria's Secret	_____	$15.00
Poison 1	_____	$15.00
Poison 2	_____	$15.00
Hell Razor Honeys	_____	$15.00
Hell Razor Honeys 2	_____	$15.00
A Hustler's Son	_____	$15.00
A Hustler's Son 2	_____	$15.00
Black and Ugly	_____	$15.00
Black and Ugly As Ever	_____	$15.00
Year Of The Crackmom	_____	$15.00
Deadheads	_____	$15.00
The Face That Launched A	_____	$15.00
Thousand Bullets		
The Unusual Suspects	_____	$15.00
Ms Wayne & The Queens of DC **(LGBT)** _____		$15.00
Paid In Blood	_____	$15.00
Raunchy	_____	$15.00
Raunchy 2	_____	$15.00
Raunchy 3	_____	$15.00
Mad Maxxx (4th Book Raunchy Series) _____		$15.00
Quita's Dayscare Center	_____	$15.00
Quita's Dayscare Center 2	_____	$15.00
Pretty Kings	_____	$15.00
Pretty Kings 2	_____	$15.00
Pretty Kings 3	_____	$15.00
Pretty Kings 4	_____	$15.00
Silence Of The Nine	_____	$15.00
Silence Of The Nine 2	_____	$15.00
Silence Of The Nine 3	_____	$15.00
Prison Throne	_____	$15.00
Drunk & Hot Girls	_____	$15.00
Hersband Material **(LGBT)** _____		$15.00
The End: How To Write A _____		$15.00
Bestselling Novel In 30 Days (Non-Fiction Guide)		
Upscale Kittens	_____	$15.00
Wake & Bake Boys	_____	$15.00
Young & Dumb	_____	$15.00
Young & Dumb 2: Vyce's Getback _____		$15.00
Tranny 911 **(LGBT)**	_____	$15.00

By ***KEESHIA K.***

Tranny 911: Dixie's Rise **(LGBT)** _____	$15.00
First Comes Love, Then Comes Murder _____	$15.00
Luxury Tax _____	$15.00
The Lying King _____	$15.00
Crazy Kind Of Love _____	$15.00
Goon _____	$15.00
And They Call Me God _____	$15.00
The Ungrateful Bastards _____	$15.00
Lipstick Dom **(LGBT)** _____	$15.00
A School of Dolls **(LGBT)** _____	$15.00
Hoetic Justice _____	$15.00
KALI: Raunchy Relived _____	$15.00
(5th Book in Raunchy Series)	
Skeezers _____	$15.00
Skeezers 2 _____	$15.00
You Kissed Me, Now I Own You _____	$15.00
Nefarious _____	$15.00
Redbone 3: The Rise of The Fold _____	$15.00
The Fold (4th Redbone Book) _____	$15.00
Clown Niggas _____	$15.00
The One You Shouldn't Trust _____	$15.00
The WHORE The Wind	
Blew My Way _____	$15.00
She Brings The Worst Kind _____	$15.00
The House That Crack Built _____	$15.00
The House That Crack Built 2 _____	$15.00
The House That Crack Built 3 _____	$15.00
Level Up **(LGBT)** _____	$15.00
Villains: It's Savage Season _____	$15.00
Gay For My Bae _____	$15.00

(**Redbone 1 & 2** are **NOT** Cartel Publications novels and if **ordered** the cost is **FULL** price of $15.00 **each. No Exceptions**.)

Please add $5.00 **PER BOOK** for shipping and handling. **Inmates** too!

The Cartel Publications * P.O. BOX 486 OWINGS MILLS MD 21117

Name: _____

Address: _____

City/State: _____

Contact/Email: _____

Please allow 7-10 BUSINESS days before shipping.

The Cartel Publications is NOT responsible for Prison Orders rejected!

NO RETURNS and NO REFUNDS.

NO PERSONAL CHECKS ACCEPTED
STAMPS NO LONGER ACCEPTED

GAY FOR MY BAE   241

CPSIA information can be obtained
at www.ICGtesting.com
Printed in the USA
LVHW03s0206130718
583547LV00001B/43/P